THE DREAD SOUTH

# Afterand City

A FRANKENSTEI
RETELLING

# ABERNATHY

## A FRANKENSTEIN RETELLING

### A DREAD SOUTH TALE

## SIRIUS

THE LAUGHING MAN HOUSE PUBLISHING

ABERNATHY

Copyright © 2025 by The Laughing Man House

ISBN: 9798999624710

www.LMHPUB.com

Case Cover Design by Mitch Green

Jacket artwork by Luisa Leiroz

Edited by Janus

Interior Design by mgsdesiigns

Illustrations by Shrike

*For Link, my perfect monster. I love you.*

*For Janus, I love you, and I hope I get to write with you forever.*

# CHAPTER ONE

*A* gator dragged the pale, puffy body all the way through the black Mississippi mud and dropped it at Ramsey Abernathy's doorstep. And the rub of it all was, this wasn't the first time.

As far as the body went, there wasn't much left for him to salvage. The head was crushed like an eggshell and the right arm was a pile of ribbons, held together by a single stubborn tendon that had served as the gator's tether. The left arm was still good, however, and there had to be some usable organs left in that bloated bag of a stomach. As soon as Ramsey picked up the good arm, his yellow rubber gloves came back covered in red-brown slime.

It was part and parcel for living so deep in the bayou. Bodies were dumped here all the time. A heavy rain was bound to wash up a few bones from the abandoned church cemetery that rested only about a mile behind his house. There were snakes and gators and herons—all sorts of carnivores that did their part to keep the water clear of useless, wriggling prey. The bodies, however, were his responsibility.

And the gators knew it.

Ramsey didn't mind. The spongy flesh offered no resistance to his bone saw and the shoulder pulled free from its joint with a little aid from his boot. He took a moment to examine the arm, testing all the fingers and the mobility of the wrist before setting it down and moving on to the stomach.

Three clear plastic liner bags layered together served to hold anything else he could salvage. The liver wasn't in bad condition, and neither were the kidneys. Everything else was brown and tight with gas, so he left it undisturbed.

Ramsey picked up the bags and twisted them closed. He picked up the arm with the other hand and then started the short journey up sagging wooden steps to his front door.

*'Part and parcel. Parcel up the parts.'* Once he was inside, the smell of death overtook every other scent in the home. His burning sticks of cut cedar and Palo Santo let off enough smoke to sting his eyes. The bright citrus wash on his wooden floors made his nose tingle and the  damp air from his churning window-unit made his long brown curls spring uncontrollably from their tight, braided knot. But death stayed at the forefront—rank gasses and putrid flesh.

Thank Christ for deep freezers.

He had to do a little bit of rearranging. There were instances in the past where he had been forced to tape his freezer shut due to a pile of disheveled body parts, and he really didn't like what that did to the aesthetic of the kitchen. Dirty, taped-up freezers made him look *poor.*

Everything else was neater than a pin, and for good reason, so anything disheveled or hard-worn stuck out like a sore thumb. Like his mother, Ramsey took a great deal of pride in keeping a clean home. He never had visitors, but that wasn't the point.

She liked to ask the question *'if Jesus showed up at your doorstep, would you be ashamed to let him in?'* And even though Ramsey had left Jesus hanging at Calvary Church, that mantra had taken tangled roots in his heart.

He also had a chemistry professor, once, who liked to tell him that *'science is messy'.*

*That* sentiment had been thrown out as quickly as it had been handed to him. Science *could* be messy. It didn't *have* to be. Ramsey didn't like to work in absolutes.

*'Any eyes today?'* His string of thoughts was interrupted by the soft, raspy voice of his brother's ghost—a voice like a tree branch scratching a glass window.

The brother whose bones were still at the bottom of the bayou. Twenty years ago felt like only yesterday.

"No eyes," Ramsey responded out loud. If anyone looking in heard him talking to his dead brother, he was sure there'd be a straitjacket with his name on it. "A liver and kidneys."

The ghost made a hissing sound like a storm door closer. *'I want eyes.'*

4

"I won't let you go blind." Ramsey stood over his chest freezer and continued to rearrange bags of assorted organs and body parts, some of them covered in ice crystals to the point where they were almost unidentifiable. He had two heads at the very bottom, but one was in dubious condition, and the other's eyes had not kept very well. "You want *all* your parts to be working, don't you?"

The ghost moaned. Ramsey leaned over the side of his freezer until he was doubled over at the waist, taking ice cube trays of blood and plastic containers of teeth and pushing them into an icy corner to make more room for a bagged pair of feet.

*'My eyes were...'* the ghost's voice tapered off. Ramsey pulled a chunk of ice off the freezer's wall and tossed it over his shoulder.

"Green," he supplied the answer after a minute's pause. It wasn't *entirely* the correct answer, but it was a simple one. Ramsey's eyes were a stormy mixture of green and grey, always reflecting one more so than the other depending on how the light hit them. His brother's eyes had been brown, just brown— *like dirt n' mudpies,* as their mother described them. The seeds of jealousy had started there. Ramsey wasn't going to let go the chance to turn things around, although he still had to establish *somewhat* realistic expectations. "Although the

5

chances of finding you one working green eye, much less two, are very slim. Less than two percent of the population has a high enough concentration of lipochrome and melanin to produce—"

The ghost hissed again, and Ramsey shut his mouth. He finally pulled himself out of the freezer and slammed it shut, pleased that the lid closed a bit easier this time than the last few.

*'I'm cold,'* the ghost whispered.

"No, you're not," Ramsey said. "You can't feel temperature yet, Wisp."

*Wisp.* His brother's ghost had appeared to him for the first time as an eerie blue light across the swamp. Ramsey used *Wisp* because his brother was dead, and his name was engraved on a tombstone somewhere in Hatchett Head. Until there was a new body, there wasn't any need for a proper name. Wisp might not want to keep the old one, anyway. There was no telling what might worm its way into a person's head, especially when it was new.

Or maybe, in this case, *gently used.*

*'You'll be working tonight.'* There wasn't any room for argument, although Wisp's voice was starting to sound like it was being filtered through a radio. Eventually, it would scramble and fade out with an electric *blip,* much like a lost signal. It would come back around, more

than likely as soon as Ramsey was elbow-deep in a chest cavity.

"I am close to a breakthrough," Ramsey muttered, speaking more to himself than the fading haunt. "I just need a little bit more time."

More time. More parts. Wisp had to know patience. Even though Ramsey could barely give that to himself.

Ramsey had never been good at naming things, and the Tank was no exception. He just called it what it was—a six-foot aquarium he bought off a saltwater fish breeder for less than it was worth. It was two feet deep and filled just a little over halfway with cloudy white petroleum jelly. The aquarium had not come with a proper lid, so he draped a few layers of mosquito netting over it just for the sake of keeping out pests.

The Tank was set up in the mudroom next to a deep, wide sink and a retired operating table that had been shoved up against the wall. It was close quarters, but Ramsey had opened things up a bit more by taking down the door that had previously sectioned off the spare room from the kitchen. Being able to keep the deep freezer accessible but out of the way was crucial in preserving his sanity.

If only it was possible to keep the house cold enough that he could leave assembled pieces on the operating table, instead of having to lug them back and forth.

His current progress was being made on a torso. He wanted a narrow ribcage, so he had harvested a smaller one, removed the breasts and sewed up the skin underneath. The nipples were not necessary nor salvageable at this stage, so he threw them out with the old tissue.

He used fishing line soaked in iodine for his sutures. In medical school, he worked hard to master his stitches so that they were as close and invisible as possible. He had been told by many professors that he had an impossibly precise hand. Of course, such praise was seldom and hard-won. His stitches were not controversial, so they *could* be praised—unlike his later work.

The torso had a few broken ribs, so he took his time pulling any shards out of the meat with a pair of tweezers and collecting the bigger pieces that could not be set back into place. Then he ground up the bone and mixed the powder in with plaster before re-forming the missing bits and leaving them for a day to dry. All the while, the torso sat on top of several gas station bags of ice, pried open like a crawfish. He brushed the skin with gum turpentine to try and make it last, but the heat had its own way of eating through every precaution.

The innards, of course, would all have to be placed in last. Right before he was ready to sew everything up and submerge his creation in jelly. Nothing that had been inside of the torso was salvageable, anyway. Most of it had been torn out by an alligator.

Tonight would be for attaching the legs. It had taken Ramsey almost two years to find a pair of similar lengths. Both needed a great deal of detailed work done to them, and only one had a foot still attached. He revitalized them the best he could, trying to *at least* get them to the same stage of decomposition. He fed a line through them both and plumped up the skin with alternating IV bags of salt water and denatured alcohol. The skin of the right leg was dark grey and mottled with soft spots like a bruised apple. The skin on the left leg was slightly jaundiced and a lot tougher, more like pale leather left out too long in the sun.

He attached them at the hip anyway. Ramsey only pulled himself away from his work long enough to put Tennessee Ford on the record player. When he returned, he took his time stitching rotten muscles and wrapping withered veins. Even breathing through a white

9

bandana wrapped around his face and nose wasn't enough to spare him from the smell. His yellow rubber gloves were coated again in dark, viscous brown.

He grafted new, healthy cartilage onto old sections and fortified it with resin. Nothing was outside of experimentation, wasn't that just it? And his past attempts at restoration had ended in complete disintegration.

By the time he was finished with his task, the record had stopped spinning, and the sun was so far gone that the only light came from a combination of the swinging yellow bulb above him and the bright fluorescent lamp attached to his head. Ramsey pulled off his headlamp and groaned. His head pounded, and now that his eyes were no longer focused on stitching and grafting, the beginnings of a headache were starting to form behind his eyes. He grabbed his gloves and pulled them off before resting his hand against the back of his neck and grabbing his chin to crack it both ways.

He looked down at his work, and he hated it.

The legs were far too uneven. Whatever measurements he thought he had he must have taken down while drunk. The old blood smeared all over the thighs would need to be scrubbed off, if he could do so without taking up sheets of skin at the same time. The open torso attached made the entire monstrosity look like an upside-down water bug with its legs sticking up. No head, only half an arm dangling off the right shoulder and a quarter of another stuck onto the left. The singular foot was turned all the way to the side and just sat there with its black toes pointing towards the curtained mudroom window.

Ramsey drew his hand across his brow, unsure of whether it was sweat or blood getting smeared into his hairline. He decided that he didn't care. It was already taking every ounce of self-control he possessed not to throw the entire rotten project into the bayou.

It had taken him a *long* time to find a satisfactory torso; else it might have been a different matter.

It was time for a break. Ramsey stuffed his hands underneath his work and lifted it off the operating table. With nothing filling the chest and gut, it was surprisingly light, although the new legs made it more awkward than before. He set it back down onto the sagging bags of ice-turning-water and left without flipping off the light.

He needed a beer, badly. And if he was lucky, then Wisp wouldn't bother him for the rest of the night.

# CHAPTER TWO

Ramsey liked sitting on his porch at night. He enjoyed the way the water reflected the stars on a cloudless night, making the line between earth and heaven blurred to seamlessness at its peak. The illusion was only interrupted by the ring of hunched cypress trees standing watch along the bank. They reminded him of turkey vultures the way they sat there, huddled. Although trees were far more vicious carrion eaters than any vulture, because eventually, a tree's roots and soil would use up *all* the parts.

He sipped his beer and stared at his own dirty fingernails pressed against the can. They weren't the hands of a surgeon, not the way he had been trained to scrub them until they were pink and to keep his nails too short to collect grime. They were a gravedigger's hands with shiny callouses and deep cracks. The irony was not lost on him, although it made his chest burn.

Ramsey pressed the rim of the can against his lips and tilted his head back for another mouthful. Two beers in and he still wasn't tired enough to sleep. One more beer after this one, and his head might be fuzzy enough to at least let him pretend. He could lay in his bed, stare up at the ceiling, and watch the rotating fan blades stir up dust until his eyes sank shut. If he was lucky, he wouldn't dream.

*Some chance.* He crunched in the sides of his beer can and leaned forward until his elbows rested against his knees. A bubble made its way up from his gut and passed through his lips without much ceremony.

Bayou Braillard was the Hell he had almost escaped. Miles of green-clotted swamp he had poured out of his boots before high-tailing it to Georgia for medical school. His mother had wanted him to go to the college in New Orleans so badly that she went behind his back to apply for him. But by the time they sent out that acceptance letter, he was already halfway to Augusta.

He'd hoped to stay there, in that rented second-level apartment of a poorly divided house. Rent was $400 and he split it down the middle with that blond-haired, blue-eyed, trust-fund baby Hudson, the brilliant brain attached to a pink mouth capable of shattering every commandment.

Ramsey missed him, even if it wasn't enough to dream about him. Baby Boy Hudson was probably shaving down noses out in California and never spared a thought for sunsets spent with bare feet against a warm wooden porch deck, swatting mosquitoes and sharing a bottle of peach Schnapps.

Although in Baby Boy's defense, Ramsey tried his best not to think about it, either. It brought up too much anger, and too much resentment towards Wisp, specifically, that wasn't fair to harbor. Even when Wisp was still flesh and bone, it wasn't his fault that he got shot. He wouldn't have wanted Ramsey to come home, if he'd had any kind of say. Ramsey did all that for their mother, because she was vomiting and crying when he picked up his phone, and every recorded message piled in his answering machine was just a series of agonized screams.

She pleaded, *'can you come home?'*

He answered, *'I'll check my schedule.'*

Because he hadn't yet told her that the hospital in Augusta had let him go.

With his brother gone, she wouldn't have cared anyway.

If Ramsey leaned over his porch railing far enough, he could see the pier buried behind an overgrowth of tree branches that was still stained with his brother's blood. All these years later and it never washed away. That was Braillard. Dirty. Bloodstained. It held onto things.

So it never surprised him that Wisp stuck around. Only that their mother had been able to move on first. Maybe there was someone waiting for her in the light on the other side. Maybe it was Ramsey's father, or Wisp's. Or the father of those three babies buried about a mile down the bank.

The beer was getting to him. Ramsey straightened in his chair and cracked his neck. Everything clicked, from his neck to his shoulders to his wrists, all the time. Baby Boy once asked, *'do you have any collagen?'*

And Ramsey's answer was simply, *'mind your business'.*

That was the last he would allow himself to think about Hudson for the rest of the night. Going to bed drunk and depressed was bad enough without adding horny to the mix. Honestly, he couldn't remember the last time he'd jerked off. It wasn't really comfortable, with his dead brother's ghost floating around.

His neck hurt. His back hurt. His whole head hurt. He thought about getting another beer just to avoid laying down and having to deal with both restlessness and pain. When he walked inside, he tossed his empty can into the trash and then glanced at the fridge just for a few seconds before he kept going. He ended up in bed, anyway, with a pillow shoved between his knees and another one pressed against his lumbar region. Neither of them really helped much, but it was the illusion of support.

The fan spinning above his head trailed ragged grey cobwebs through the air like they were birthday streamers. Footsteps paced outside his bedroom door, back and forth, heavy and petulant.

He thought about getting back up to do some more work, and then he fell asleep.

offee was the smell that pulled Ramsey's face away from his pillow. Bold and invigorating, but not at all fresh. He knew without having to walk all the way to the kitchen that there was none brewing. And it made sense, after all. He was the only house occupant who could boil water and start the pour-over.

Wisp's inability to grasp things rendered it no better than a poltergeist. But it liked to knock the coffee bag over in the kitchen, as if the knowledge that Ramsey Abernathy would do almost anything for coffee still remained as one of the spirit's core truths.

Ramsey rolled onto his side and slid out of bed. There was no point in fighting for ten minutes more of sleep. He walked into the kitchen and picked up the crumpled coffee bag from the floor before doing anything else. The top was open, and a good fourth-cup's worth of grounds had spilled. Ramsey rubbed his face and scooped the mess up in two big handfuls, dumping them into a glass jar by the sink. His grandmother saved her coffee grounds and eggshells and fed them to her window plants.

Ramsey didn't have plants, but he couldn't stand the waste regardless.

A streak of color caught Ramsey's eye; blood on the linoleum—a thick, reddish-brown drag mark with handprints streaking through. He froze with flecks of coffee still stuck to his palm and his eyes followed the path all the way towards his operating room.

"Wisp?" He had to take a deep breath to keep from growling. "What the fuck were you playing in last night?"

Ramsey dragged his hand down the side of his bed pants and walked towards the mudroom, watching his step so that he didn't accidentally set his foot in a slick puddle and go flying. The handprints were erratic, as if his brother's ghost had fallen and had to scrabble to get up. At the end of the bloody path were the mangled remnants of the body he had been working on only hours before. Most of his precise seams had been ripped apart and the remains were left to fester on sagging, bloated bags of water that used to be ice. Some of the bags had sprung a leak and there was water all over the floor, creating greasy rust-colored pools where it ran into the blood. A loud, resonant burping sound went off right next to Ramsey's ear and he jumped.

"You goddamn *rude* piece of shit!" Ramsey scrubbed at his face with both hands. "If you

18

don't like where it's going, you need to *tell* me!" He looked around for his yellow gloves and found them hanging over the side of the mudroom sink. He pulled them on just so he wouldn't have to touch the body with his bare hands. Well, it was useless now. Hours of work spent tenderizing gator food.

*"Not right."* Wisp's voice was crackling grease popping on a stovetop. *"You didn't get it right."*

"I would like to know what I *have* gotten right." Ramsey kicked a mostly empty white bucket closer to the mess to start dumping shreds of skin and shattered limbs into. They splashed dirty mop water when they hit the bottom. "These materials are not easy to come by, and this is the third project you have completely trashed. All these years wasted and, at this rate, I won't have anything left to give you."

*"I want **mine**,"* Wisp said. *"My body. My eyes."*

"The minnows at the bottom of this godforsaken swamp ate those a long time ago, honey," Ramsey hissed through his teeth. "I couldn't put your skeleton back together if I had an instruction manual and a whole tub of hot glue. Half of your bones have probably been carried over to the next county by now. You are going to have to *drop it.*" Ramsey started picking up the plastic ice bags that were already mostly empty and set them in the sink to finish draining. "You need to be fucking *realistic.*"

Wisp made a pathetic sound like a sick kitten. It took everything Ramsey had to not punch the wall in front of him. He settled for picking up the white bucket and letting it swing from his fingers while he walked out onto the porch.

As he passed the window above the kitchen sink, he caught a glimpse of Wisp in the reflection. Squirrely and tall, trailing Ramsey so closely that it could be mistaken for his shadow.

Ramsey slipped on his black rubber boots with mud caked around the soles before descending the front steps. He made it all the way down to the edge of the bank, watching his step for anything that might be writhing around in the mud, before he pulled the body parts out and tossed them into the water. Each one landed with a dull, flat *splash.*

Finally, he poured the dark grey water out of the bottom and then turned back towards the house.

Starting all over. He hadn't even had his morning coffee yet, and now he would have to drag out his sketchbook for some inspiration.

A cold snap overtook his lungs. Ramsey couldn't breathe and he clutched his throat, stopping dead in his tracks to try and heave out a deep breath.

*"There!"* Wisp's voice was like banging pots and pans. *"There, there, there, there!"*

"Shut up! *Can it!*" Ramsey snapped. He whipped his head around, looking in all directions for whatever the hell Wisp was seeing that he wasn't. As far as he could tell, there was nothing, except for rapidly gathering packs of clouds so dark grey they were almost green.

*Hurricane season.* "I'm going inside," Ramsey said.

If Wisp was sulking, he didn't care. Ramsey stomped up the wooden steps and dropped the bucket at the door. He put his mind on a shower, then coffee, *then* he would drag out his sketchbook. In reality, he knew he probably wouldn't get as far as the shower without the gears in his brain turning towards possible improvements on the never-ending project. But at the very least, he could use that time to think.

Even if Wisp tried to talk to him some more in the shower, since the ghost had such a poor concept of privacy, the streaming water would block it out.

# CHAPTER THREE

**B**y late morning, the rain was just starting. Ramsey turned on his radio for weather updates and ended up on a local Blues station instead. That suited him just fine. He grabbed his big calfskin journal, its pages overburdened by sketches, diagrams, and scribbled notes his grandmother would have compared to chicken scratch, and he set it down on the kitchen table next to his steaming coffee cup. It was his third, and the brew was starting

22

to taste bitter—a little too acidic and a little too watery, but he bore it just for the sake of going on. The pages of his journal crackled when he turned them over, weighed down by ink and stained heavily with water and years' worth of brown coffee rings.

Wisp scratched at the kitchen window, its nails like naked branches rattling against the glass. Ramsey pinched the radio dial and turned it up as high as it could go to drown out the repeated battering. He didn't know what it was the spirit wanted and he didn't care. Ramsey didn't have a dog because he had tried to avoid putting himself in this exact situation. But who needed a dog when you had an obnoxiously needy, dead brother?

He tried to keep his attention on his notes. *Something* in them would hold the answer. All these years studying, examining, practicing...he had to have already cracked the code, it was just a matter of putting the right pieces side-by-side. Even if he had a body that Wisp liked at this point, he could not guarantee that he would be able to animate it properly. Sure, there was the Tank, and the jelly, and the car batteries and the jumper cables and the grates and all the little fine copper wires that could be jammed deep into the flesh. But it was all theory, still, it wasn't concrete science. The closest he had come to success with that method was getting a dead frog to flip back onto its belly and croak once before giving up the ghost yet again.

And he refused to count it as a success because the damn thing wasn't *still* alive. It only mattered if it lasted longer than thirty seconds, and according to his notes, it hadn't gone past fifteen. Any short-term bout of electricity could tease a dead body into jumping up and throwing a kick. But to give it back *life* was something else, entirely.

He wasn't after life eternal. It wasn't like he was trying to bottle up immortality and sell it to billionaires with a big golden string. For some reason, at this point, that sort of goal felt far more achievable. Life *prolonged* was a whole different game because it was already there. Everything was still in working order and you just had to keep it from failing. But to get it all going again after it had rotten down to almost nothing...

Ramsey plunged his fingers into the corners of hie eyes, trying to dig out the exhaustion before taking another big gulp of coffee. With Wisp still scratching at the window, he was tempted to give an ultimatum. *'If you don't stop fucking do that, you can forget about a new body.'*

It wouldn't have worked, or he'd try it.

Ramsey leaned back in his chair and wrapped his hands around the sides of the coffee cup. He didn't care that it burned and made his palms tingle. The faint, stinging pain was all that kept him from flying into a dozen pieces with each new scratch at the window.

What would his mother say, if she were here? *'Be nice to your brother, Ramsey. Just give him what he wants so he'll stop making a fuss.'*

That very mentality had stuck to his brain like chiggers and followed him throughout his life. Doctor California Baby Boy had said something similar, once. *'Just tell the board what they want to hear, Ram. They'll leave you alone if you do.'*

*Scratch. Tap.* Ramsey took a deep breath and drummed his fingers against the sides of his mug.

"Wisp," he finally cracked. "What the hell is it?"

The scratching stopped. Ramsey flickered his eyes over towards the kitchen window now covered in a thousand fine, shallow lines.

*'Ramsey,'* his brother's ghost whined. *'They're perfect eyes.'*

Oh dear God in Heaven. Ramsey set his mug down and stood up from the table. "It is pouring outside," he said. "I am going to drown if I step off the porch wrong."

Like Wisp cared. Ramsey wasn't even sure if the ghost remembered enough about what it was like to be alive to understand why Ramsey

25

would go out of his way to avoid dying. Or spraining his ankle, or hurting his wrist. If something turned the wrong way or popped out of place it could easily be a month of recovery for him. He was a slow healer.

And then his great work would be delayed even further.

The scratching started up again. Ramsey stomped towards the front entrance just to stop himself from throwing his fist against the wall. He grabbed his rubber boots and ripped his rain slicker off its hanger. He shoved his face up against the door and tried to take stock of the situation through the peephole, but of course his luck wasn't that good.

"This body of yours better be within arm's reach," Ramsey warned. "Or I'm coming right back inside."

The body in the swamp was in bad shape. Somehow, it had gotten caught underneath a cage of cypress tree roots with its limbs twisted in all directions. There was no telling how long it had been there, or how Wisp had taken notice of it at all. Nothing, except for the long black hair still attached to what was left of the scalp, was visible above the surface of the water. Some of it was just bone, but one of the eyes was still intact. It was a stunning aventurine green, while its twin was concealed by a thick cataract that left it whiter than a marble. Ramsey figured he would harvest both, just to be safe—and there was always a chance he could remove the cataract on his own. Even if he had to throw that one out, that left him with *one* green eye. The perfect shade of green, even, which was more than he had to begin with.

Despite the battering rain, he set to work sawing away a few of the roots that stood between him and his prize. They were thicker than he realized, and his small handsaw was not very strong. By the time he reached the body, his arms and shoulders were sore. He created enough of an opening to reach through with both hands, bracing the skull with one hand and setting the teeth of his blade against the corpse's neck with the other. He figured he might as well take the whole head. There was no way he was going to get both eyes out cleanly from such an awkward angle. And, who knew? The head could probably be salvaged as well. There were large patches where some of the existing skin might have to be cut away and replaced, but that was overall not as bad as it could have been.

While he worked his saw back and forth, he grabbed as much of the tangled black hair as he could and wrapped it around his hand. It was useful to grip and wrench around, also, to help break the neck faster and separate the head completely. The swamp water churned around his elbows and the rain battering against his slicker sounded like *Bang Snap!* poppers going off around his ears.

Finally, there was some give, and Ramsey's elbows shot back towards his chest as the head came off its neck. He wrestled it through the interlaced roots before finally holding it up to give it a proper look. It was more damaged than he thought, but it still didn't matter. Maybe alive, it had even been a handsome face. He had to wonder how it ended up here so close to his home, what creature or man had been responsible for its demise. The body was so fresh that there was no way it had come from the old cemetery. The evidence of what had been done was no doubt lurking underneath the water, but Ramsey was not curious enough to go looking.

Off the neck and waterlogged, the head *had* to be a good ten pounds. Ramsey carried it with his fingers on one hand still locked into the soaking black hair while the other braced the stump, holding everything together the best he could. He took the head back into the house and set it down on a stretch of butcher paper.

For the first time in a *long* time, there was the feeling of joy in the house.

# Chapter Four

Wisp's excitement was infectious. By nightfall, Ramsey was inspired to return to his work, except now he needed another torso. And the one he had pulled the head from, if it was still caught in the same place, was without a doubt in too bad a condition to be useful. There was a chance that the cemetery would have what he needed, but it was a long haul in the dark after a storm.

Although his brother's ghost would not understand and did not care.

And if Wisp was pacing around the house all night, scratching and whining in that raspy wind-sucked voice, Ramsey was not going to get any sleep.

It was pitch-black outside after the storm died down, with still enough cloud-cover to keep the moon fully shuttered. Ramsey threw a flashlight to his traveling pack (even though he was already wearing a headlamp), before also adding a rolled-up, homemade blue tarp body bag for anything he found. His hopes weren't high in terms of a trunk that had been preserved well enough to get any use of, but setting out and digging for himself was better than sitting at home and twiddling his thumbs at the kitchen table.

The tarp stretched over his family's airboat had an excess of water pooling in the center, and it all went running down the sides the moment he started messing with it. The water splattered against the already-drenched ground around his feet, creating a veritable sinkhole where Ramsey's rubber boots tried to get stuck. He folded up the slick tarp as small as he could and stuffed it down into the boat, since he didn't have a better place to put it that was within reach.

Ramsey boarded the boat and dug two foam earplugs out of his pocket, pushing one into each ear. He jammed the key into the ignition and started up the engine, making a face at the sudden roar of the whirring propeller. Even if he didn't intend to go *fast,* it was damnably loud. It didn't help that the muffler had fallen off some time ago and he had never bothered to get it replaced.

The beam from his headlamp shot a white circle of light onto the water in front of him, which wasn't much, but it was *something.* He did have electric boat lights somewhere, but there was a very good chance they weren't even charged.

He wished he'd have thought to bring his radio, but he wouldn't have been able to hear it anyway. Besides, even though he didn't have much by way of neighbors, he wasn't too keen on drawing any more attention to himself than he already was.

The only thing louder than the boat's propeller was the chorus of chirping frogs that hit its crescendo right as

Ramsey closed in on the bank near the old church. He wondered, idly, what hymns they were singing and if God found their voices endearing. The church had seen better, no doubt, for a one-room building wedged so deep into the mud that its foundation had turned to sludge and yet, it still stood—as white and sharp-edged as ever, covered in weeds and climbing vines. Maybe it fed off the songs of cicadas and bullfrogs, the swamp's own angels like seraphim and cherubim clustered around the throne of the Almighty.

The iron fence around its cemetery was not nearly as inaccessible. It was only as high as Ramsey's ribcage with big enough spaces between each bar for him to wedge the toe of his boot in. He was able to set his boot against a rung and then swing his leg over the top, carefully keeping his hand between the spikes along the top to avoid slipping and becoming speared. He came down hard on the other side with his pack sliding along his shoulder and dragging him towards the ground.

As soon as he landed, Ramsey set the pack down and dug out his extra flashlight as well as the short-handled shovel he had brought. He left the pack on the ground and then pushed the button on his flashlight to cast its wide beam across the cemetery floor. Alongside his headlamp, it gave him a good amount of light—

which was useful, above all, because he had no wish to get bitten by a snake.

The ground squelched underneath his soles as Ramsey crept between the headstones. Most of their faces had been weathered down, with their inscriptions barely legible and covered in algae and mildew. More than half of the stones were broken or dislodged from the constant flooding, and the eroded graves in front of them had been turned inside-out. Now they were just giant sinkholes waiting for new, unwitting bodies to occupy them.

On the far end of the cemetery, a giant weeping willow tree bent over the iron gate and draped its leafy green curtain across as many of the graves as it could reach. The headstones caught up in its net were in better shape than those surrounding, even with their graves mostly intact. Ramsey wondered if it had anything to do with the roots of the tree itself, if they were tangled around the coffins and holding them down, prying apart their sides and feeding on the meat like black walnuts. He kept to the perimeter until he closed in on the tree and only then did he dare to walk closer. He kept having visions of stepping on top of a sinkhole and vanishing into the soft earth's mouth, sucked down like crawfish ripped from the shell. Underneath the willow, the ground was firmer—more trustworthy. He kept his flashlight moving from headstone to headstone, searching for any inscriptions that caught his eye. Off to the side, there was rustling suggestive of thrashing tails and long, writhing bodies moving through the overgrown grass. He tried not to dwell on it.

Ramsey finally came to a stop in front of a leaning headstone. There was nothing special about it; he wasn't sure what caught his eye, except for the fact that it was one of the cleaner headstones and likely one of the newest. The inscription was perfectly legible, but it just read "Singing with the Angels" without a name or a date underneath. But the grave was intact, or at least it seemed that way as far as he could tell, and it was good a place to start digging as any.

Ramsey set his flashlight down and placed the tip of his shovel against the dirt. Because of the recent rain, it was soft and loamy, not *quite* like shoveling mud but close. He piled it up beside him and kept working past his arms screaming at him for soreness. It didn't take much for his body to start rebelling. A little protest from his wrists and shoulders was no reason to give up.

The singing bullfrogs and buzzing mosquitoes were the white noise that slipped him into a trance. Ramsey lost all track of time and didn't stop digging until the point of his shovel struck wood. All at once, the bullfrogs fell silent, and the only sound in his ears was a high-pitched ringing. Ramsey's fingers ached like they were going to fall off. He sank down to his knees and brushed his hand across the dark, damp dirt—revealing the lid of a wooden coffin underneath.

*Coffin, not casket.* He knew the difference. This one looked old, so there was a good chance he was wasting his time. In the incandescent light the wood appeared red, like a nice dark cherrywood. There were some pale gouges across the lid, almost as if a shovel had scraped its surface before. Ramsey frowned and cleared some more of the dirt away. Was he losing it, or did the gouges in the wood form patterns?

To him, they looked like double-ringed circles filled with S-shaped curves and inverted triangles chiseled out by crude tools. Some of the finer scratches looked like letters, but nothing that came together to form legible writing. He ended up taking off a glove and pushing his fingers into his eyes to try and clear up some of the fuzziness. They were probably markings from digging creatures or grave robbers of the past. Nothing to do with him and certainly nothing that *meant* anything. He was seeing things, but brains were like that—willing to try and make sense out of scratches and dents.

Ramsey kept digging, even though he already knew what was inside. It would be skeletal remains, or less, and he wasn't there for bones. He needed revivable tissue he could breathe a little life into. He needed flesh that he could flay apart and wrap around his brother's ghost like a new coat. He needed muscles, skin, *organs.*

And yet, he couldn't bring himself to stop.

The nails holding down the lid were rusted and offered no resistance when Ramsey pried it open. He threw his arm over his nose before the lid was even fully up, anticipating the stench, but to his surprise he wasn't met with the smell of rot. Instead, it was earth, and faintly dried rosemary and dill.

But that was far from the worst of it. The body in the coffin was not long-dead at all, in fact, it looked *fresh.* It had been buried completely naked with its head shaved and a sachet around its neck—which was what he assumed the herby smell was coming from. The leather thong holding the sachet in place rested on top of a purple ligature mark, which made the cause of death look like strangulation by a wire or a rope—up until the dark, deep imprints like thumbs that rested right underneath the chin, on top of the windpipe.

Ramsey swallowed hard, suddenly too aware of his own breathing, which somehow made it difficult to draw in a full deep breath. His sense told him to slam the lid shut, throw the dirt back onto the coffin, and leave the cemetery altogether.

On the other hand, it was exactly the size torso he had been hoping for, and in such excellent condition he would be a fool to leave it untouched. The damn thing looked like it was still warm. He couldn't feasibly take the *entire* body with him, although he considered it for half a moment. He took off his other glove and rested both hands against the body, just to reassure himself that the corpse was, in fact, cold. He still half-expected to pick up a heartbeat.

Nothing. It was just a regular body, and he was working himself up for naught.

His hand saw was in his pack, which was all the way across the cemetery. He would have to trek back, retrieve it, and return to claim his prize, but it would be worth it. Even if it took him until dawn, having his hands on such a perfect specimen would catapult him that much closer towards his goal.

He half-expected the body to be gone by the time he retrieved his tools. Yet, it was still there, laying belly-up in its cherrywood coffin like a dead catfish. A drop of rain hit his nose, which was all the warning that Ramsey needed to finish what he had to do, and quickly. He slid his rubber gloves back on.

It took 45 minutes to saw through all the limbs about a quarter of the way down and then take off the head. Another fifteen to roll the torso up in a cheap plastic shower curtain and then drop it into his homemade body bag. After putting all his tools back into his pack, he hauled up the bag and gripped it tight with his gloved fists as he walked back towards the iron fence.

Ninety pounds, his conservative estimate. He was used to lifting and hauling, even with his bad back and his hips—even with knees that started firing off skull-splitting pain signals if he went too long without something to lean on. He had a cane, his grandfather's, that he thought to himself he should have brought. He hadn't because it was just one more thing to carry.

Thankfully, with the fence not being terribly high, he didn't have to lift the body bag very far to get it over the top. He split the action into two and braced the torso against the fence to give him some leverage for the second heave. It landed on the other side with a heavy, crinkled thump. Meanwhile, the rain was picking up, and the iron bars were slick.

Ramsey's boot slipped as he was climbing and his leg turned at an awkward angle. It dragged against one of the spikes across the top and a flash of pain down his shin made his head reel as he fell.

When he landed, Ramsey sucked all the air he could through his teeth to keep from swearing aloud. He looked down at his leg, and his headlamp lit up the bright red blood soaking through his pantleg. Pain pulsed up to his ballooning knee, already pressed so tightly against the stiff fabric around it that bending it was nearly impossible.

*Excellent. Incredible.* He didn't want to be caught belly-crawling towards the water. That was just asking for tragedy. He couldn't go still and lay there, either, because not only were his chances of being found nominal—but if someone *were* to stumble upon him and try to help, then the chopped-up body in a hand-sewn tarp was sure to raise some questions.

*'You shouldn't have come here.'* Ramsey could berate himself all day, it wouldn't change his situation.

Something slithered across his leg. Ramsey almost didn't catch it. He pushed himself up onto his elbows and glanced down just in time to see a long yellow tail with brown spots like a banana peel slip off his pantleg and vanish into the grass. He started to jerk his leg back and then flinched at the same time, anticipating another nauseating wave of pain.

Except, there was no pain. The deep laceration was still pumping blood, but it had gone completely numb. Ramsey's heart sped up at the realization, but he still wasted no time in taking off his shirt and tightening it around the wound to staunch the bleeding.

The *thing* he had just seen looked too long to be a salamander. His money was on something closer to a snake. But then again, snakes did not have poisonous skin like some salamanders, and he didn't know what else could have that effect just by brushing over his skin.

And if there were toxins already seeping into his blood…

The tingling in his lips and fingertips had to be purely psychological. At least, that was what he told himself. Ramsey managed to push himself up onto his feet, even though his injured leg wobbled, and used the temporary relief to his advantage to get back to the boat. He dragged his pack with him first and tossed it over the side. Then, with a surge of determination, he grabbed the edges of the body bag and hauled it down the bank, barely managing to get it up into the boat.

His leg gave out as soon as he sat back down. But at least he could set the boat towards home, and then he could worry about possible blood poisoning.

# CHAPTER FIVE

'*H*eal me, O Lord, and I will be healed. Save me, and I will be saved.*'*
Ramsey never thought about the pertinence of the crocheted verse, framed and still hanging over the stove where his mother left it, until he had his leg propped up on a kitchen chair and the guts of a First Aid kit strewn across the table. Bandages, isopropyl

alcohol, and needles that were hardly medical grade—but they got the job done.

He used red fishing line instead of clear to sew himself up because he wanted to be able to keep an eye on the swelling. The wound was still numb, but he had no other symptoms of poisoning since returning home, so he decided he was fine. A quick shower and half a bottle of alcohol poured over the wound made him feel better. Besides, the nearest hospital was over forty-five minutes away, too much of a trek for something he could easily take care of on his own.

The torso was still wrapped up in its body bag on the kitchen floor. He had pulled it in and dropped it like luggage. It had taken every bit of strength he had left just to get it up the stairs.

Wisp hovered nearby. Ramsey saw its reflection in the dark face of the microwave. Man-shaped, but fuzzy around the edges.

*'What is it?'* The edges of the body bag crinkled.

"Don't touch it," Ramsey growled. "I just cleaned up the mess you made with the last one."

More defiant crinkling, like a cat rustling a plastic bag. *'What last one?'*

"Leave it alone. If everything goes well this week, then you will finally have the body that you need." Ramsey tucked in the edges of the white bandage wrapped around his calf and then used both hands to pull his leg down from the chair.

*'Tonight?'* Wisp's voice cracked like radio static.

"I need some rest first." Ramsey gestured to his leg. "I went through a lot to get this for you."

The kitchen cabinets flew open. Ramsey jumped and then closed his eyes, pinching the bridge of his nose while his heart settled. Dishes came flying out—cups and plates and bowls, all plastic. He had cleaned up enough broken ceramic in the past to not have to learn that lesson twice.

*"Cut that out!"* Ramsey slammed his hand down onto the kitchen table. The raining plastic clattering onto the floor stoked his rage like a bellows and it took every bit of restraint he had not to hurl something at the cabinets.

*'Tonight!'* Wisp's voice climbed, the squealing of an adjusting radio. *'Tonight, tonight!'*

"I'll put this on ice," Ramsey nudged the bag with his foot, "but that is as much as I am going to do."

Heavy silence, and then, *'you're a bad brother.'* The voice sounded so clear, so much like the person it had once belonged to, that Ramsey almost fell off his chair.

That did it. He stood up, setting his hand against the kitchen table to keep himself steady with one knee trembling.

"Let me find grandaddy's cane," he said. He didn't get a response, but he preferred the silence to the slamming and banging.

His grandfather's cane was all wood except for a brass L-shaped handle anchored to the shaft by a pin. Ramsey dug it out of his mother's closet where it was still concealed behind stacked boxes and plastic bins all these years later. The room still smelled like her, like clean laundry and *Passion* perfume—the half-filled amethyst bottle for which was still sitting on her dresser. Ramsey lingered just long enough to glance over at her bed—a chipped white metal frame and an old, hard mattress covered in a worn white bedspread with soft pink flowers dotting the fabric. It appeared perfectly cozy, like it was ready for her to sink into after a particularly long day.

She had died in that bed. Ramsey had done everything he could to make it look as if nothing ever happened. But there was no amount of sweeping and mopping that could draw her presence out of that room. Mildred Abernathy's memory lingered, stronger than her lost son's feeble ghost.

The door to her attached bathroom stood wide open, baring the divide where wood floor changed to shell pink tile, the change marked by a brassy aluminum threshold bar. Ramsey was at the right angle where he caught his own reflection in the mirror above her sink. He was so used to seeing Wisp in odd surfaces that it didn't take him by surprise so much as disturb him when he realized it was his own face.

Had his cheeks always been this hollow? And those dark circles under his eyes, had they always looked like bruises? How long had he been this tired, this drained, and did his hair always look so matted—or was it because he had not washed it since digging up a new body for his brother?

Gripping the cane tightly, Ramsey let it bear his weight while he walked into the bathroom. The mirror was attached to a medicine cabinet, which sprang open as soon as he touched the side. The cabinet was still cluttered with all the little things he had meant to clean out and never did. Crumpled boxes of bandages, a handful of cotton swabs trapped in yellowing plastic, a half-filled bottle of hydrogen peroxide.

A white crocheted angel no bigger than his palm, stuffed into the top corner.

And three orange pill bottles. Two of them were empty, one had about five or six pills left in the bottom. The RX label on the front had his mother's name printed right above the drug and dosage, although the ink was smudged.

MILDRED ABERNATHY.

TAKE AS DIRECTED.

PERCOCET. 10 MG.

Ramsey plucked the bottle off the shelf and turned it around in his fingers. He rattled the pills around and considered them through the orange plastic. Did he really need a painkiller? That little push would probably be enough to get him through the night. And being past the expiration date, it was a gamble as to whether they would even work. He ran through the list of side-effects in his head even as he twisted off the cap. *Dizziness. Confusion. Nausea. Vomiting. Fatigue.*

He placed one of the pills on his tongue and turned on the faucet. He ran his hand underneath it and carried up two mouthfuls of water until the bitter pill was down.

Ramsey turned the water off, replaced the cap, and slid the pill bottle into his pocket. Maybe it would be worth it, maybe not. But his mother didn't need them, anymore.

He took one last look in the mirror. *Dark circles. Beard scruff. You probably smell like you look.*

He turned away and left the bedroom altogether, dragging the door shut behind him.

A tall barstool in the corner of the kitchen had once been used to hold flowerpots and family pictures, the work of a console table but for folks who weren't in a high enough tax bracket to know what that was. Now, the stool found new employment in keeping Ramsey's busted leg off the ground while he set to work on his creation. Between that and his grandfather's cane, he figured he could manage.

The Percocet was, miraculously, doing its part as well.

Ramsey figured he could get in a good 4-5 hours' worth of work before he started to feel it. He dropped the needle on his Hank Williams record then started by taking the newly acquired torso out of its bag and laying it out on the operating table. He wiped it down with antiseptic wipes just to see what he was working with, to see what the skin looked like now that it was underneath a proper light and no longer covered in dirt and hair-like roots.

It was a little bit worse than he thought, but that was almost a relief. Once everything was clean he went digging for the rest of what was needed. Arms, legs—everything perfect and accounted for down to the fingers and toes. He pulled out bags of frozen organs and set them in the mud sink to start thawing in case there was anything he needed. He didn't want any surprises.

He started on a Y-shaped incision down the torso to investigate the state of things inside. Most of the organs were dark and bloated, which sent a new wave of paranoia washing over him. With a body that had been dead for a while, he would expect things to be more shriveled-up. The bloating suggested that they had not been dead *long,* but then again, the *when* wasn't really his problem as long as they *were* dead. They were on his table, now, so he had to force himself not to dwell.

The hours ticked down his aching vertebrae and he felt every single one like a chiming grandfather clock. He only realized how much his eyes hurt when he had to look up and dig for a new spool of fishing line. His yellow gloves were caked in so much blood and wood glue, which he used to bind broken bones together, that he had to take them off so he could sew. By the time he finally felt like he could place the head, there was so much blood under his fingernails that he could have scraped it out and used it for a transfusion.

The head still sat on its butcher paper, which was soaked through completely by blood and swamp water. Ramsey picked up the head and gave it a good shake, wringing out the water from the tangled ends of its black hair before taking it over to the table.

It suited the body so well—almost perfectly. It settled beautifully onto the neck as if they had been joined together the entire time with the very subtlest of color gradations. It was beautiful. Gorgeous. Stunning. Ramsey couldn't have been happier and he didn't want to examine his emotions too closely, with joy and delirium being so similar. He cinched the throat together extra carefully with his tiniest, tightest stitches. After all this time, he was so close, so close to the end of the road.

He had no idea what time it was. The sky was still dark and rumbling, but there might have been some light trying to peek through the churning clouds outside his small workroom window. Another round of storms and rain, and it was just as well. Had he tied down the boat properly? Had he left anything outside that was in danger of getting swept away? He couldn't remember or bring himself to care. The Hank Williams record had ended and was just spinning away, the needle scraping at nothing.

Ramsey straightened his back long enough to pull up the tonearm on his turntable and he glanced at his work. It looked so much like a *person* that he almost jumped back. Up until that point it had just been parts—stitches, glue, skin, and teeth. But now, as a whole, it looked like a man sleeping on his operating table.

His heart raced and Ramsey rubbed the center of his chest. The Percocet was wearing off and his head throbbed like it was going to roll right off his neck. The pressure from the storm wasn't helping, he was sure. He had come so far in a night, or a day—however long it had been. He never thought he would reach this point. He barely remembered the plan.

But it wasn't done yet, either. It wasn't ready for the next phase. Ramsey flipped over his record to let the other side spin. Forty-five more minutes, he could get through that.

# CHAPTER SIX

Ramsey worked into the early afternoon, and by that time, most of the touches he made were cosmetic in nature. He attacked the mess of black hair with a brush, a comb, and a mess of hair cream he pulled out from underneath his mother's bathroom cabinet. It was a lot wavier than he initially thought and more difficult to detangle. He ended up cutting the worst of the matts and covering them up with longer sections before putting everything into a thick braid. He cut away a section of skin across the face that had an unsightly rash and sewed on a new piece that did not *quite* match, but was as close as he had available. He trimmed, filed, and picked until he was satisfied. At the end, he decided to leave the eyes as they were. Eye surgery was a delicate procedure, and he was beyond the point of exhaustion.

Ramsey dragged himself back into the kitchen and let himself collapse into a chair. He was disgusting, he *knew* he was disgusting, and too tired to even think about making a cup of coffee to perk himself up. Ramsey leaned his head against the wall and closed his eyes.

'STOP THAT!' A shrill shriek like an ambulance wail pulled him out of his near unconsciousness.

"What?" Ramsey rubbed his face and shuddered at the residue on his hands. "I have to sleep." He glanced over at the microwave where Wisp was pacing back and forth, moving so quickly its form looked like a bat flying across the reflective door.

'You're. Not. Done!' The microwave door pulled itself open and then slammed shut. Ramsey ground his back teeth and fought against the anger piling up at the base of his aching skull.

"No, I am not done. But I need to sleep. If I keep going like this, I am going to make a mistake." Ramsey stuck his hand down in his pocket and fingered the prescription bottle cap. Another dose would knock him right out. Painless, for just a few hours. "I haven't even touched the eyes. Don't you want me to make them perfect?"

*'THEY. ARE. PERFECT!'* Wisp twisted the hot and cold knobs next to the kitchen faucet so that they let out panicked squeals. *'THEY. DON'T. NEED. ANYTHING! Make it!'*

"Make it…" Ramsey rested his head against the wall again. "*Just make it, Ramsey.* You don't even know what you're asking. You're a rotted brain and swamp gas. You don't remember being tired, or hungry, or hurt."

*'I remember you.'* Hissing steam. *'I remember what you did.'*

Ramsey's chest burned again. He tried to breathe past it.

*'You're a bad, bad brother. Bad, bad, bad!'*

"Stop!" Ramsey pulled himself upright. "Stop, stop, okay—let me make some coffee. I need to make some coffee and take my pills."

The faucet knobs continued to squeal and groan as Wisp wrenched them from side to side, but the ghost was quiet otherwise. Ramsey ignored the squealing used the already-running water to fill his kettle.

He tried to out the *'what next'* in his head, but nothing was coming up. Nothing except pain, and frustration, and all the bitter angry thoughts like throwing the kettle against the wall when it whistled and pulling the faucet off the sink to stop its shuddering. And then all he could think was, *'it's probably time for the Tank.'*

The Tank—it was already full. Full to the brim with petroleum jelly, and all he had to do was put the body inside and stick some stripped wires into all the nerve bundles.

One crank from the generator, maybe two, and if nothing happened he could go to sleep and try again. But maybe that would be enough to convince Wisp that science shouldn't be rushed. Goddamn haint didn't know anything about...

Hot coffee splashed onto his foot and made Ramsey shout before sending him into a dance. He hadn't even realized he was already holding the coffee, but the pour-over pot was full, and the scalding water burning a hole in his foot was brown. Ramsey set his mug down and threw a towel onto the tile before picking the mug back up and leaning over the counter to take a sip. His hand shook, but whether it was from exertion or pain, he didn't know.

'*What next?*' The coffee burned his tongue and the roof of his mouth, but he didn't stop drinking.

He could wheel the operating table over to the tank and then it would only be a little bit of lifting. Lowering the body might prove tricky, but maybe there were some straps laying around...

Ramsey left his mug on the counter and went back into the workroom to see what he could find.

he body was still on the operating table when he returned. Ramsey wasn't sure what else he expected. He grabbed swaths of mosquito netting and wrapped it around his hands, dragging it off the top of the Tank while he considered every movement it would take to drop the body into the jelly. Once the netting was off, he figured he only had a few minutes, if that, before airborne pests driven in by the rain started taking a nose-dive into the stuff.

If he was going to be successful, there had to be as few variables as possible, down to the smallest housefly.

Ramsey grabbed the sides of the operating table and paused. He was forgetting *something*, he just didn't know what it was. He thought that he had checked off every box. He ran down the list in his head, but the words were all jumbled, the boxes jumping around and squeezing the checkmarks out like goo. *Jelly.* He looked down at the Tank for inspiration.

He walked away long enough to grab a pair of army green forearm straps, and then it hit him. *He hadn't checked the brain.*

Of course. He had been so careful about everything else. Yet he hadn't even once cracked the skull open to peek inside and see what was there. If anything *usable* was there. Did he have a brain stored, if this one was full of holes or covered in tumors? What kind of brain was locked inside this comely head, hand-picked by his dead brother's ghost—was it even one worth salvaging? After all, the person who it once belonged to couldn't even keep themselves alive.

Ramsey swore under his breath and went to grab his tools. Every movement felt too agonizingly slow. He had to watch his own feet as he stepped over bags and tarps, trying not to trip and fall on his face. The surgeon inside of him who had completed all those rigorous years of medical school scowled at the mess. A proper doctor would clean up after himself. A proper doctor wouldn't let the work environment become so hazardous.

A proper doctor would have done a craniotomy before considering the whole project done and dusted.

New gloves. Incision. Drill. Skin pulled back, rolling down along the forehead like drawn-up shades. *Buzzing,* the sharp, high-pitched squeal of whirring metal against bone.

*Elevate the fragment.* Ramsey braced the loose piece of skull with his fingers and drew it back, carefully. The inside of the cranium was completely black, and a thready mesh of what looked like fungus clung to the piece in his hand. Ramsey furrowed his brow and leaned in closer, sweeping his gloved fingers carefully along the thick edges. His fingertips came back with black dust smeared across the yellow.

At first, he thought the cavity was completely empty. But when he stuck his hand in again, it hit something solid. Ramsey furrowed his brow and scooped at the sides, working his way around to try and get a better look. The brain, or whatever was sitting where the brain should have been, was stiff around all sides, with only a little bit of spongy give at the very top. Ramsey pushed his fingers in a little deeper, and a big chunk split from the rest, creating a white tear across the surface. He took his scalpel and used its tip to flip the chunk over, getting a glimpse of white flesh and then crimson gills underneath.

The gills themselves glistened like they were wet. Ramsey pressed the flat side of his scalpel against them, and watched as thin red liquid burbled up around the edges. His stomach turned and he dropped the scalpel, plunging both his hands into the brain cavity and digging out as much of the black fungus as he could. He set it down in hunks on the metal tray that held his tools, afraid some of it would get into the tank if he started throwing it towards the floor.

A brain. He needed a real brain. He had one, didn't he? Sitting in a jar somewhere, or encased in Tupperware down at the bottom of his freezer? Ramsey staggered over to the deep freezer, throwing open the lid before lowering himself to dig.

Kidneys. Livers. Lungs. Hands. Ears. *No brain.*

His hand smacked against a jar. It was buried at the bottom, wedged into an icy corner with a lid as wide as the span of his hand. Ramsey grabbed the sides of the lid and dug it out, squeezing his fingers together to act like a trowel as he chipped away at the ice. Finally, the jar came free, much bigger than it looked, and holding exactly what he needed.

A beautiful brain. He couldn't remember what he had preserved it in, but it wasn't frozen.

The liquid was briny yellow, and when he twisted off the cap, it smelled like formaldehyde. It didn't matter, though. It was all he had.

Ramsey stood up. His knees wobbled and he walked back towards the operating table.

"It's almost complete," his voice trembled, but he kept muttering to keep himself going. "It is almost complete."

# CHAPTER SEVEN

More fishing line. More needles. Once the new brain was nestled inside its cavity, Ramsey glued the piece of skull he took back into place and then had to pull the skin back over and sew up the incision. No more clear fishing line, he had to use red. His stitches weren't as tight or as neat as he was capable of. He jabbed his own fingers so many times that his blood smeared everywhere, and he couldn't bring himself to care.

His hands shook as he secured the army green straps around the body and then slipped the loops around his forearms. His arms similarly protested when he started to lift, wobbling and sending a bolt of pain down to the center of his back. Ramsey ground his teeth and pushed himself harder, wrapping the straps around his hands, using that and his forearms to pull the body off the operating table. It was something he could have done if he was better rested and if everything didn't hurt so badly.

He set the body against the side of the Tank, which did not tip over thanks to the weight of the jelly. He pulled off the straps, and it was *that* motion that caused his shoulder to slide and dislocate. Ramsey let out a growl and pushed the body over into the jelly with his knee, grabbing his shoulder and popping it back into place while a white haze bloomed over his vision.

Some of the jelly swelled up to the top rim and spilled over the sides of the tank. It dripped down the glass walls, the same cloudy-white as spunk. It smelled similar, too, although Ramsey couldn't tell if that was the jelly on its own or all the scattered body parts, warming and decaying in his workroom.

He grabbed the battery, the cables, the wires. Thunder shook the sides of the house and the lights above his head flickered, but he barely spared it a thought. He had the generator. He wasn't worried about the power. The body had landed face-down in the Tank, which gave him access to those nerve bundles all clustered-up at the spine. Ramsey plunged his hands down into the jelly and drove the wires into the soft, deteriorating skin. Every breath felt like it was being squeezed out of him, but he couldn't stop. He was so close.

The power flickered again, right on the heels on another roar of thunder. Lightning sizzled just outside the windows, as bright as a nuclear blast and louder than a gunshot. As close as it was, Ramsey figured that it must have struck a tree.

The body sat at the bottom of the Tank, enclosed in petroleum jelly, and Ramsey cranked the generator.

More thunder. Another bolt of lightning. This one was even louder, and it made the house shake like the walls were going to start coming down. The lightbulb above his head exploded and set fragments of glass raining down to the floor. Ramsey's fingertips tingled. His mouth tasted like pennies and his ears rang with white noise. He kept his eyes fixed on the body, looking for any sign of success. Any twitch, and jerk.

And then he saw it. The left index finger moved, he was *sure of it.* Then again, and another finger, and then all the fingers on the left hand curled inward. The right leg twitched, then jerked.

The left hand opened and slammed against the side of the tank. Ramsey rocked back on his heels and fell, landing on his ass. His vision blurred again and his head spun, but he still watched as the hand slid up the glass and the other arm came down, searching for support.

The head. *The head moved.* It lifted its face up and the mouth opened, just a little, like it was searching for the surface—*trying to breathe.*

"You're alive," the words got caught in Ramsey's throat while all the euphoria rushed to his head. "You're alive, you're alive—*Victor, you're alive!"*

Victor. The first time he had said his brother's name since he was lowered into the ground. It sprang victoriously off his tongue, and was swallowed by an enraged shriek that filled the room.

*'LET ME IN!'* Wisp's voice—why was he still hearing Wisp?—was garbled and fried, the sound of rocks being slammed against concrete while being ground against one another. *'Won't let me in! What have you done?'*

"What do you mean?!" Ramsey screamed to be heard over the noise—over Wisp's shrieking, over the rain pelting against the windows, over trays and jars and tables being overturned and thrown against the wall. Over the thrashing of that *creature* in the tank, desperately trying to get a grip against the glass, enough to stand up.

'*Get it, it's going to drown*' was the only thought he could form.

Ramsey crawled over to the tank, keeping his head down to avoid getting hit with the objects of Wisp's tantrum.

'*WHAT HAVE YOU DONE?*' Wisp's voice melded with the overhead clap of thunder.

Ramsey couldn't answer. He reached into the tank and wrapped his arms around the creature's chest, hooking his forearms underneath its armpits before hauling it back. The jelly sucked at his arms, fighting him every step of the way, until the creature's head broke the surface and its chest heaved against his hands. He heard it take its first coarse, wet breath.

"It's alive." Ramsey's vision started to tunnel and those were the last words to escape his lips. "*It's* alive...!"

And then his vision went black, and the world was finally quiet.

When Ramsey opened his eyes, it was dark, and something was touching his face.

He didn't know how long he had been laying there on the workroom floor. He was laying on his bad shoulder, but the pain had settled into a dull ache that crept up his neck and knocked against the base of his skull. The hand, at least what *felt* like a hand, against his cheek was wet.

Ramsey blinked, and his eyeballs squelched behind his lids. When he opened them again, his sight adjusted a little better, and he was able to make out the face across from his, resting against the floor atop a massive, coiled braid. The one dead, milky eye didn't seem fixed on anything in particular, while the aventurine green one was largely obscured by shadow.

The creature let out a hard exhale. Its foul breath skated over Ramsey's face and he knew that it was, indeed, a living thing.

Terror struck him in the belly, driving out the last few traces of elation that lingered on the tail of his victory. And even *that* small sense of success was spoiled with the knowledge that he had not held the proverbial door open long enough for his brother's ghost to take hold. But he couldn't do it over, could he? He would have to do it *again.*

Which meant that the creature he faced now was a stranger to him entirely. Impressionable as a newborn, covered in slime as if fresh from the womb. The creature let out another breath and Ramsey made a face. He pushed himself up into a sitting position, despite his arm screaming at him, and the creature started to rise as well.

Ramsey held out a hand and gave the creature a hard stare. It looked back at him, that singular green eye shining through the darkness like it was lit from behind with a lantern.

"Can you speak?" he asked. The creature continued to stare at him.

Ramsey's hand started to shake, but he kept it up. He raked the other one down his face, tugging at the corners of his mouth with his thumb and forefinger. "Well, you are not Victor," he said. "You are nothing close." Ramsey had never been asked to name anything. It went so far as his stuffed animals when he was small were just referred to by their species with only slight variations, names like *'brown dog'* and *'black cat'.* Even *Wisp* was taken from his mother's talk of *will-o-the-wisps* wandering through the swamp with their eerie blue lanterns held high. Ramsey was not creative in that sense and never claimed to be.

But it didn't feel entirely right referring to this sad, wet thing as just *Creature*. It was mostly man, after all, the first of however many it would take. The first man created by Ramsey Abernathy's hands.

"Adam," Ramsey tested it out. The first man, a bit cliché, but who was going to say anything about it? "I suppose you look like an Adam."

Adam tilted its head. In the darkness, it reached for him and caught his hand. It slid its fingers between his own, and for a split second, their palms came together.

Ramsey felt its heartbeat through its hand, and he drew back as quickly as if he'd been burned.

"*No*," Ramsey said sharply. It was like correcting a dog, he decided. Well, now he had two. Adam looked hurt, although the room was so dark that its mangled face was difficult to read. Ramsey could still see the harangued expression through that downturned green eye.

He was in no condition to deal with that sort of hurt, kicked puppy attitude. He desperately needed a shower and a change of clothes. He needed something on his stomach other than coffee and he needed five to six hours of real sleep. In the meantime, there was no telling what this *thing* would get into. It would probably take three steps out the front door and drown.

Ramsey grabbed the side of the tank and gripped the rim tight, pulling himself up carefully while trying to avoid slipping through the mess of jelly on the floor. His cane was sorrowfully far away—closer to the door, and so of very little use. The creature's head moved, and the only way he could tell that it was looking up at him was by tracking the one eye.

"You have to get up," Ramsey said. The creature either couldn't understand him, or its brain was still leaking chemicals and could not yet turn electrical pulses into a cohesive thought. Ramsey thought about offering his hand, but he wasn't risking his balance.

"*Up,*" he tried to simplify it. He braced himself against the wall and reached down to grab the creature's shoulder. He pulled up on it, but without much force, just enough to urge and give the idea of what he meant. He gestured up and down, the same motion he had used to rise. "*Up.*"

Something seemed to click. Adam lowered its head and grunted, an awful sound that made Ramsey cringe. It pushed itself up onto its knees and then started to gather its legs up to stand. It didn't get very far off the ground before it slipped and crashed back down against the tile.

It might have landed on its face; from the way its head bounced in the dark and there was a solid *'smack'.*

Maybe Ramsey didn't have to worry about it finding its way out the door.

"Try again." He didn't reach down this time. Instead, he extended one leg very carefully and nudged its ribcage with his toes. *"Up."*

Adam let out a long, hard breath. It pushed itself up on its arms, grunting again with the effort, and mimicked Ramsey's motion of grabbing the sides of the tank. Ramsey kept an eye out in case the tank decided to topple, now that it was less full. Against all odds, the creature managed to stand. It extended its arms and stood perfectly still for what amounted to thirty seconds before it let out a little pleased chirp.

If standing took this much, then walking was going to be worse. Ramsey didn't have that sort of time or patience. He held up his hand again, palm flat towards the creature. "Stay," he said. He half-expected it to follow him anyway, but it did not. It stood in that same spot, arms spread outward like an image of Christ staggering out of the tomb. Ramsey managed to cross the slick tile and get all the way to the doorway to grab his cane. The tile was dry, if somewhat sticky, closer to the kitchen. As soon as he reached the entrance, Adam whimpered.

"Don't." Ramsey turned around and walked back with surer strides, relying on his cane to keep him steady. "We're not going to start that." He pushed himself up underneath the creature's armpit, wrapping an arm around its chest and forcing it to lean on him for support. The creature wobbled a bit, and Ramsey grit his teeth, willing himself to stay upright. He wasn't any sort of praying individual, but he considered picking it up where he had left off at age eleven just for the sake of not dislocating more than his shoulder.

Once they hit the kitchen, Ramsey felt far more in control. He adjusted himself underneath Adam's armpit to give it a bit more support, and then he redirected them towards his mother's bedroom. Placing such a gross abomination inside what had become his mother's shrine felt anachronistic. But it was only temporary.

He lowered Adam to the floor. The creature's legs folded up and its knees splayed out awkwardly where it sat. To Ramsey, it looked like a fawn that had been dropped on its hindquarters.

There still wasn't much light. Ramsey flipped the switch on the wall and nothing happened, so he made a note to check the generator. He kept his eyes on the creature as he stepped over towards a low dresser and began rooting through the top drawer. He found what he was looking for—a single coiled leather belt that had belonged to his grandfather, and then he shut the drawer again before moving back towards Adam.

Ramsey's creature looked up at him, but he didn't meet its gaze. He wrapped the belt around its neck and buckled it around the white metal post at the end of the bed. He slipped two fingers down to make sure it was loose enough for the creature to breathe, and then he pulled back.

"If you pull too hard, your head is going to fall off." Ramsey said, with no idea whether that was true or not. Anything was possible. "Do you understand me?"

The creature didn't make a sound until Ramsey pulled away, then it started whimpering again. Ramsey grumbled in his throat but didn't bother to go back and discourage the behavior, he just shut the bedroom door.

# CHAPTER EIGHT

The power came back on as soon as Ramsey started peeling off his grimy, gore-soaked clothing. He was so relieved that he didn't even question it, he just kicked his clothes into a corner and limped towards the shower where his fingers left rust-colored streaks on the clear knobs. He braced himself against the wall and closed his eyes. When the hot water hit his back, he almost broke down into tears.

Ramsey stood there for a full minute, watching the filthy water swirl around his feet and race towards the drain. He only moved when he realized he hadn't pulled his hair down, and he yanked the elastic out of it so his curls could tumble free.

A hand slammed against the mirror. He could barely see it through the aquatex shower door, but he heard it like a red brick being hurled at the glass.

"Stop that!" Ramsey pounded his fist against the shower wall, since there was nothing else to strike. "I am not talking to you until I've had some sleep."

*'Ruined!'* there was a startling clarity to Wisp's voice. For the first time in a *long* time, it sounded much more like the brother he remembered, but like his brother's voice was being thrown down a long hallway. *'Ruined it! You have to fix it!'*

"It will take time," Ramsey said. "And even then, I can't fix it before I know what went wrong."

*'Blocked. Shoved. **Pushed away.**'* Wisp hissed. *'Couldn't enter.'*

"Fascinating. I wonder why that happened." Ramsey turned around to face the shower head. The hot water on his face was beyond welcome.

It did wonders for his throbbing temples. Ramsey grabbed a bar of orange soap and started sliding it over his skin, getting into every crevice to scrub away the layers of dirt and blood that had built up from his work and from the leg wound. He slid the bar down to get between his thighs, and his slick hand brushed his cock, the brief sensation sending an electric pulse up to his brain like he'd been shocked.

Ramsey swapped the bar to his other hand and leaned against the shower wall. Even though he was standing, his back did not scream at him in the same way as it did without hot water as part of the equation. How long had it been? He was so beyond exhausted that even with Wisp tapping on the mirror and pacing, and couldn't bring himself to care about the ghost. There was some semblance of privacy, at least, with the textured door between them. Ramsey wrapped his hand around his cock, leading into an upward stroke, and it came to life almost immediately with the thick vein pulsing against his palm. Ramsey closed his eyes and started pumping, gliding his hand up and down the soft foreskin, pausing every third stroke to reach his fingers back and squeeze his balls. It didn't take long at all for an orgasm to hit him—intense enough that it rocked his hips back and sent cum shooting from the head straight towards the drain. Exhaustion followed it so heavily and quickly that he nearly blacked out again.

Ramsey paused to catch his breath and then stepped back into the shower stream, rinsing off the sudden clamminess and then scrubbing the day out of his scalp with the same orange bar before stepping out. There was nothing behind the mirror when he emerged, not that he looked too hard. He wrapped himself up in his towel and made his way to his bed even as his pain started to catch up to him by creeping up his legs.

He thought that he could hear Adam in the other room, whimpering, whining, and grunting. He elected to ignore it and collapsed into his bed instead, staring up at the fan that was back to spinning lazily above his head.

This time, it didn't take him long at all to fall asleep.

'There is someone in the house,' Wisp's voice was up against Ramsey's ear, the same pitch and volume as a blaring boat horn. Ramsey sat bolt upright in bed, already sweating from the hot sunlight seeping through his window. He ignored the pain in his legs as he slammed his feet against the floor and grabbed his still-damp towel just to have something to wrap around his waist.

He tightened the towel around his hips and stepped out into the short hallway. To his left, the kitchen was still a mess with dishes all over the floor from Wisp's temper-tantrum. Cloudy marks made by petroleum jelly dragged over the tiles and left pale splotches on the hardwood leading to his mother's bedroom. That door was still shut, thank God. He couldn't hear anything from the other side, which made his heart thump against his ribs. Did the creature die overnight? Was it sitting there, spoiling at the end of his mother's bed? With a hurricane the day before, the water would be high and rough, and the banks would be nothing but sludge. Ramsey didn't really know what other 'someone' would be in the house other than Adam...

"Excuse me," from his right, there was a voice. Gentle, unobtrusive. "This is a bit awkward, but may I use your telephone?"

Ramsey swiveled his head to look towards the front entrance. The person standing right by the open front door was as tall as he was, with long brown hair pulled back into a braid and dark brown eyes that regarded him from behind rectangular glasses. He couldn't help but take in their structure—aristocratic nose, sharp jawline, long fingers concealed by black half-gloves. Narrow shoulders, straight hips, straighter legs—the body he would have killed to acquire for his brother, rather than having to cobble one together out of stolen pieces.

Ramsey shook his head to clear his thoughts. "What?" He narrowed his own eyes. "Where did you come from?" They weren't dressed at all for the weather, no rubber boots and no rain-slicker. They didn't look like they had walked through the mud at all. They wore a white dress shirt underneath a tailored, yellow pinstripe vest over black church trousers. Instead of a tie, they wore a kerchief of the same yellow.

All the sudden, Ramsey was very aware of the fact that he was standing there in *only* a towel.

"You've never met me before, but we're neighbors," they said, gesturing behind them. "I live out in that direction. My house was broken into and now it's full of water, and I don't have any power." They didn't look very upset, the way they smiled. "So, may I use your telephone?"

Ramsey glanced over at the kitchen. He didn't believe them, but he couldn't find a good way to say 'no' either. If they just used the phone, and then left, and the creature didn't make any noise...

———————

"It's in the kitchen," he said. "Come on in." He wanted to say something such as *'you shouldn't just walk into people's houses'*, but he could already hear his mother's voice in the back of his head. He needed to be hospitable, he needed to be neighborly. She would never have turned away someone in need, but then again...she never would have put herself in a situation like this one.

He tried to think about what his mother would have to say about Adam, then decided it would be nothing good.

He was so lost in his thoughts that he didn't have the decency to apologize for the mess, or for his state. He led the stranger to the kitchen and pointed to the olive-green phone on the wall. The receiver dangled from its cord; evidently knocked off the cradle at some point by Wisp's fit. The stranger thanked Ramsey and picked the received up delicately, holding it to their ear as they dialed a series of numbers he didn't bother to analyze.

Ramsey stepped away, inching closer to his mother's bedroom door and straining to listen. He still couldn't hear anything. He had time, probably, to go find something decent to wear before showing the stranger out. But on the off-chance that Adam made any kind of noise...he just wasn't sure it was a risk he was willing to take.

Still, the towel was only going to last so long. If he could push past his pain, he could move quickly enough to recover his cane and grab something to wear and be back before the stranger hung up the phone. They weren't even talking yet, they were humming. Which, under most circumstances would be annoying, but in this case, Ramsey considered it a boon.

He dashed into his room, grabbing a pair of jeans and a green t-shirt from the floor in front of his dresser and throwing them on. They smelled like they had been there for a while, but that was the least of his problems. He could change again after the stranger was gone. He grabbed his cane and walked back out, headed for his mother's room, glancing only once towards the kitchen to make sure that the stranger was still there.

As soon as his bare toes hit the seam near his mother's bedroom door, the floor creaked, and Adam started whimpering on the other side. Ramsey's heart kicked up its pace and he put his hand over his mouth, scrubbing at the corners to try and stop himself from cursing out loud. He held his breath and turned the knob, sweeping the door open as quickly as possible so that the hinges didn't creak.

*"Shush!"* he snarled as soon as he burst into the room. The creature was sitting on the floor, now in full daylight, which did not shelter any

part of its ghastly appearance and put the full horror on display. The knotted, puffy seams, the dead white eye, the disheveled black hair, the discolored skin...it sat there, in full nakedness, the most terrible and yet stunning thing he had ever seen. Because only hours ago, it had been a pile of dead meat and shattered bones, and now it was alive. A full creature, something so close to being human—by *his* hand, and his hand alone. An act of God, *truly*, an act of Ramsey Abernathy, who was ready to challenge God for His position.

Adam, for its part, reached out for him. Its jaw trembled like it was going to cry, except Ramsey wasn't sure if his creature even *could* cry.

The way it contorted its body to extend its hand, the way it looked at him with its good eye peering through a loose strand of black hair, made it look like a real corpse. And with that realization, Ramsey was hit with the *smell.* The whole room was steeped in the smell of rot, covering up the last hints of *Passion* that lingered in the air.

Ramsey rotated on his heel, doubled over, and threw up. There wasn't much on his stomach, so it was mostly yellow bile. He heaved and wrang out his gut until there was nothing left, and when he straightened up, the taste of acid lingered on his lips.

"Are you all right?" The stranger's voice startled him *again* and Ramsey whirled around, gripping his cane. He had forgotten they were there. They were standing back far enough that he couldn't be sure of *what* they had seen, but he wasn't going to take any risks.

Ramsey grabbed the stranger by the throat and pushed them all the way back out and into the hall. He slammed them up against the wall and pushed the brass head of his cane underneath their chin to tilt it upwards.

"What did you see?" Ramsey growled. The stranger was shockingly calm, reaching up with one hand to trail their fingers down the length of his cane.

And he *knew* how hard he was squeezing their throat. He was surprised they could breathe, while their face only had the faintest hint of red.

"Is there something you don't *want* me to see?" they asked him. "Something you're ashamed of?"

Ramsey squeezed a little harder. "Something I need to protect," he said. "But *nothing* to be ashamed of. If what is in that room made it through the front door, I would be..." he stopped himself short of saying *'revered'*, and landed on, "...*applauded* within the scientific community."

Their lips curved, just a little. "I don't doubt it." They kept moving their fingers up and down.

"So, why not share it with me? Your beautiful scientific breakthrough."

"It's not beautiful." Ramsey let up on his grip, just a little. "I can stomach it, because I created it. You would most likely run screaming in terror."

"I think you would be surprised." The stranger looked at him. Their deep, brown eyes had flecks of gold and orange right where the sun hit them. Like vibrant autumn leaves floating on the water. "What if I promise you that I won't run screaming?"

"I won't let you," Ramsey said. He hoped that the hanging implication spoke for itself. He didn't want to have to chase anyone down and he certainly didn't want to have to kill anyone, but he was realizing, very quickly, that he *would* do a lot to keep his creation in his own hands.

It was true immortality. He had harnessed the power of true *life,* of *being*—it was power unspeakable, and he knew that the vultures would be waiting to discredit him, demean him, revile and expel him as they had before. He had to keep this to himself, for now, just until he could figure out how to receive his due. His laurels. And then there was Wisp—he had to do something about that, too. Wisp was the whole reason he had started down this path.

Ramsey peeled his hand away and let the stranger settle on their own two feet. He withdrew his cane and could see the imprint of his hand on their neck. For half a minute, he was ashamed of his own rage.

They stepped around him to peer into the room.

'*Devil,*' Wisp hissed. Ramsey batted the air, irate.

"I haven't eaten," Ramsey whispered, trying not to let the stranger overhear him talking to a ghost. "I wasn't thinking."

He didn't know what he expected. Screaming, maybe, or a thud as they fainted and their body hit the floor. Ramsey waited for the duration of a heartbeat and then followed. Whether it was curiosity to see their raw reaction or the need to have his innovation *seen, admired, praised*—he wasn't sure.

The stranger stood only inches away from the creature, bent at the waist with their hands resting on their thighs. Adam stared up at them, its own expression holding the sort of terror a small animal might feel in the path of a predator.

The stranger reached out and touched Adam's cheek. Adam flinched and the stranger cooed.

"I wouldn't call you hideous," the stranger said. "I think you're perfect. Handsome, even. Look at you—so much care placed in every part.

Meticulously crafted. Beautifully, wonderfully made."

Ramsey's heart swelled with pride. He moved even closer until he was standing side-by-side with the stranger.

"What is its name?" The stranger slid their fingers behind the bedpost and loosened the belt. Ramsey almost stopped them, but Adam didn't look like it was going to bolt.

"Adam," Ramsey said. "At least that is what I am calling it, for now."

"It is nice to meet you, Adam," the stranger said. They wrapped the belt around their hand and kissed the creature on its forehead. "My name is Abel."

They turned their head to face Ramsey. "I should have introduced myself when I walked in," they said. "I apologize that I was not being very neighborly."

As if it was neighborly to slam someone against the wall with every intention of choking the life out of them. Water under the bridge, he supposed. "My name is Ramsey," he said. "Dr. Ramsey Abernathy."

"Mildred's boy, I know." They flashed a smile. "She said that she had sent you off to become a doctor. Sounds like you made it."

Every thought in Ramsey's head came to a screeching halt. This person had known his mother? They did not look nearly old enough to have been her peer, especially not when he was just heading into school.

"I need to clean up," Ramsey finally said, changing the topic as he gestured towards Adam. "I need to...see if I can get it into any clothes."

"You do that," Abel said, straightening. "I'll be in the kitchen."

# CHAPTER NINE

If it was anachronistic to store the creature in Mildred Abernathy's bedroom, it was even more so to put it in Ramsey's dead brother's clothes. On one hand, this was the exact reason Ramsey had saved and stored them. On the other, things had clearly not panned out in the way he had hoped. But it wasn't as though Wisp would know the difference.

The clothing was a little loose, but objectively better than bestial nakedness. Dressing Adam was a lot like dressing a scarecrow, and the visual result was much the same.

Finally, Ramsey held out his hands. "Come on," he said. "Let's get you up."

Adam didn't seem to register the command fully, so Ramsey reached down and grabbed the creature's hands on his own, tugging to urge it up onto its feet. Adam stood, its legs still a little uncertain, but it did not need nearly as much support as the night before.

Gaining strength was a good sign. Ramsey wondered if he could get it to eat, and if that would also help. Would its stomach even be able to digest food? There was so much to experiment with, so much that needed to be documented.

Ramsey held Adam's hand and walked with it into the kitchen. The bright sunlight, not filtered through the same soft layers of curtains and blinds as his mother's bedroom, made the creature wince and throw its hand over its eyes. Ramsey watched it, greedily taking a mental tally of its every minute movement, and guided it towards a chair at the kitchen table.

It was only then that he took notice of how clean everything was. It was as if the previous night had never happened. The dishes had been picked off the floor and put away, and the floor had been mopped with the faint scent of lemon and clove lingering underneath the strong cloud of sizzling bacon and Johnny cakes.

Ramsey wasn't even aware that he possessed half those ingredients. Abel stood by the stove, flipping yellow cakes in a generational cast iron skillet with one hand and pouring coffee with the other.

Ramsey couldn't pin down how he felt about a stranger just making themselves at home in his kitchen, but his growling stomach overpowered his irritation.

"You didn't have to do that," Ramsey said. "I can cook."

"I will take that as a 'thank you' and simply say that you're welcome," Abel responded. "How is your dear child holding up to a brand-new world?"

"*That?*" Ramsey looked at Adam. "That thing is no child of mine."

Abel seemed to disapprove of that sentiment, evident in the way their mouth puckered while they cracked eggs into the same skillet that held the bacon. "You made him, didn't you? I would say that qualifies you for at least a mug. Maybe not *'World's Greatest Dad'*, but something in that vein."

"Never get attached to your own work," Ramsey argued. "That is what they teach in every discipline of science and art—you will have to take it apart, and do it over, so don't start considering it too precious to destroy."

"I wouldn't say that children are too precious for that." Abel tilted their head. "How many babies are buried in Hatchett Head? And how many just beyond those trees?"

Ramsey's gaze sharpened. He stared Abel down, even as they demurely set a full plate in front of Adam, and then him. "What do you know about that?" he asked hotly.

Abel shrugged and settled into the chair that separated Ramsey from his creation and pulled a collapsed gold cigarette holder from their pocket. They lengthened it between their fingers like a telescope and then wedged a slender, filter-less cigarette onto the end. "Your mother spoke about them, now and again," they said. The end of their cigarette sparked to life without being touched by a flame, and their nose twitched. Something about their expression made it look as though they hadn't meant for that to happen.

"Not to me," Ramsey said, folding up a piece of bacon and wrapping it up in a torn piece of Johnny cake.

"Of course, not to you," Abel said. "You wouldn't have listened." They turned towards Adam, who was just staring at its plate. They kept their cigarette away from the creature's face as they took its fork and cut the food into

92

small pieces. "Here you go." Abel scooped up a piece of Johnny cake and held it to Adam's mouth. "Take a bite, dear. Just like daddy's doing, see?"

Another flash of anger. "Don't call me that," Ramsey snapped.

Abel grinned. "What do you want him to call you? *Doctor?*" As if that was entirely ridiculous. They shook their head. "Here comes the riverboat." They swerved the fork through the air. Adam still looked confused.

"Stop that," Ramsey said. "It cannot understand what you're saying."

"I think he knows." Abel tapped the food against Adam's lips. The creature finally, slowly, parted its lips. Abel scooped the food into its mouth and then held their hand, gently, underneath its chin while it chewed.

"It's all muscle memory," Abel said. "You'll get used to it."

"You're very candid with a corpse," Ramsey said dryly, taking another bite of bacon and Johnny cake together. "I'd kill to know what skeletons you have in your closet."

"I have no secrets." Abel scooped up more food onto Adam's fork. "I'm an open book. Most just don't ask the right questions."

"Have you ever killed anyone?" Ramsey asked. It was an absolutely unhinged question to ask a stranger, he was well-aware. But the circumstances of their simple breakfast were far from orthodox to being with.

Abel waited until Adam took another successful bite and then said, "I have facilitated a few deaths. Not nearly as many as I have simply witnessed."

Ramsey's heart kicked up again. He couldn't tell if it was from excitement, horror, or something in-between. "Is your background also in medicine?" he asked.

Abel looked like they were mulling it over. They fed Adam another bite and then swept their thumb over its face to wipe off a few crumbs. "I admire surgeons more than I emulate them," they finally said. "When your mother said you were going to become a doctor, she had so much confidence in that statement that I knew she believed it to be absolutely true. And she would have given anything for your success."

Hearing about his mother made his chest tight, but Ramsey wasn't ready for the conversation to stop. "She said something like that to me, once," he admitted, trying hard to fight back the tears that pricked the back of his eyes. He was *not* going to cry in front of a stranger, no matter how much they talked like they knew him already. "She told me that she had spoken to God, and that she would pray for my success every day. She told me that..." he trailed off. He couldn't finish.

Abel smiled gently. "She wanted you to be famous," they said. "The most famous surgeon, that was what she said."

"I failed in that," Ramsey said flatly. He looked over at Adam, the creature that brought him so much hope and such a deep sense of failure at the same time. He clung to his pride, because that was all he had. He would make *something* out of this, even if he had to disassemble his own work piece by piece and start it all over again.

"Not all successes are linear," Abel said. Then asked, sounding amused, "spoke to God? Is that what she said?"

Ramsey shrugged. "Something like that. I think she phrased it as 'called in a favor with the King'. That was just her way, how she talked about things. Her relationship with God was so personal, like she could walk with him and talk with him as they did in Bible days."

Abel nodded, as if that was satisfactory, and turned their attention back to Adam. "Is it bringing anything back? The more you listen, the better you'll be able to speak." Abel tucked tendrils of Adam's hair behind its ears, as if they couldn't keep their hands away. "Do you have books?" The question was addressed to Ramsey.

"Texts, I think," Ramsey said. "I kept everything from school…"

"No, real books—fiction, something that will open up those lovely chambers." They tapped Adam's forehead.

Ramsey crinkled his brow. "My mother left behind some novels," he said. "Romances, mostly." Teaching that thing to read was not at the top of his list, but he supposed it wouldn't hurt, eventually. It all depended on whether or not he decided to keep it.

"I think that will do," Abel said. "It is not a bad start. Ah, look at you!" They moved Adam's plate closer. The creature was using its fork, emulating the way Abel had been feeding it. Its movements were a little awkward and stilted, but it was eating on its own.

"That is excellent," Abel showered the creature with praise. "Look how quickly you are learning! Soon your *doctor* won't be able to keep up with you."

Ramsey grunted and finished his food.

"I have some cleaning to do," he said.

"That's fine," Abel told him. "Adam and I will just be with your books."

# CHAPTER TEN

'*Devil.*' Wisp had been absent all through breakfast, and didn't make its presence known until Ramsey was deep in the process of cleaning up his workroom. Its accusatory hissing sounded like steam from a broken pipe.

"I need to document the process and the results," Ramsey said. "Tomorrow I will see what I have left, and what I need. Once the water level goes down a bit more, there may even be some new material to work with."

*'Eyes,'* Wisp moaned. *'Perfect eyes.'*

"I will recycle the head," Ramsey reassured. "You can keep your perfect eyes."

That seemed to appease the ghost. Ramsey filled up three difference trash bags and knotted them at their necks. He sponge-mopped the floor and righted the overturned tables, wiping everything down with blue disinfectant and a rag.

He would refill the Tank later. For the moment, he focused on scooping out all the old jelly and cleaning the stuck bugs that had accumulated overnight from the glass.

"The bayou takes care of us," Ramsey said, to no one in particular, although he was certain that Wisp heard. He was finding that to be particularly true, not just in how he had been able to collect so much, but in how it had delivered help right to his door.

Up until this point, he had done everything on his own. And despite never having peace, or privacy, and always having a demand that needed catering to, Ramsey was alone. In some ways, he felt like he always had been, like he had been born into negative space.

He wasn't about to look a gift horse in the mouth. Things were bound to turn sour with this neighbor, eventually. But until then, Ramsey would hang onto them for all they were worth.

Once he was finished with the cleanup, Ramsey went searching for Adam. He found it in the living room with Abel—a room so rarely used in the house that the lampshades had collected a horrendous amount of dust.

His mother's romance novels were spread all over a low coffee table, while Abel and Adam both sat on the floor. Abel had one book cracked open until it lay flat and was dragging their finger underneath the neatly printed lines, sounding the words out and encouraging Adam to mimic the sounds. Ramsey stood in the doorway and watched them—watched Adam's mouth struggle to make shapes and work in tandem with its tongue. Abel had a seemingly inexhaustible amount of patience, from the way they would walk back their finger and sound out the same word, again and again, while Adam made sounds like a dog with a bone shard caught in its throat.

He was only able to tolerate a few minutes of that before Ramsey turned away and looked longingly towards his bedroom. God only knew, he would have loved a little bit more sleep. With Wisp quiet and Adam occupied, it seemed like the ideal opportunity. However, he wasn't keen on leaving his house unguarded with a stranger, *especially* one so available and friendly.

Because a ten minute window would be enough for Abel to take Ramsey's witless creation and slip out the front door. And in the expanse of the storm-tossed wetlands, it would be an impossible hunt.

Ramsey returned his attention to the scene and saw Abel in the same position, but looking right at him. Their leaf-brown eyes sparked red, while they never moved their finger from the line of text that Adam was paying such close attention to.

"Doctor Abernathy," Abel said, "why don't you sit down with us?" Their voice was warm, inviting, and Ramsey found himself moving from his position before he had really registered what they were saying.

"I have some work yet to finish," he muttered as a weak protest. Ramsey chose a worn recliner that was wedged into a corner near a tall reading lamp. It was far enough away from the pair that he felt he could get comfortable, but close enough to observe.

"Of course," Abel agreed. They turned back to the pages spread out in front of them, and Ramsey rested his cheek against his knuckles. His eyelids sank and his attention drifted, beyond Adam's clunky vocalizations and Abel's gentle, patient directions.

He didn't mean to fall asleep, but it found him anyway, swallowing his vision and his consciousness both in one numbing gulp.

Sleep held Ramsey down and refused to let him get out of the chair, but his dreams were lucid enough that he was a little *too* aware of his state. It was like sleep paralysis, but a little bit worse. He saw himself sleeping and was startled by how waxy and *dead* he looked. For one panicked second, he thought that he had died in his sleep, but his chest was still rising and sinking and his eyes still fluttered behind their lids. Ramsey hovered by the chair and watched himself breathe until he was absolutely sure he wasn't gone, and only then did he start to walk around.

A shadow flitted across the wall, followed by a hideous clanging noise. It sounded like it was coming from the room right across from Ramsey's...his dead brother's bedroom. Ramsey hadn't stepped foot in it since the funeral, not even to clean. Part of that could be blamed on his mother. She hadn't wanted him to touch or move anything. After her death, it was just totally lost as a priority. Ramsey mostly kept the door shut because he was certain it was full of German cockroaches or something, at this point, and he didn't want them escaping.

Ramsey stood in front of the door and flattened his palm against it. His hand phased right through the wood and he stumbled forward, hopping over the threshold to keep his balance. In his dream, he didn't ache as much, and his steps were strangely light.

As soon as he straightened up, Ramsey was hit with the smell of decay—recognizable even buried underneath piles of mildewing, unwashed clothes and blankets that hadn't been laundered in years. There was food litter stuffed into every corner—brightly colored chip bags, half-empty soda bottles, and crumpled tinfoil—and the bed was likewise covered in debris. Mostly old papers and photos their mother had once sorted through, and dead bugs. Lots of dead bugs.

Victor sat on the edge of the bed. *Not Wisp,* Ramsey felt in his gut, *Victor.* He wasn't sure what the difference was to his subconscious, what marker stood out enough to propel that decision. Victor looked just like Ramsey remembered him best—young, eighteen or nineteen, with short, frizzy brown curls and mudpie eyes. He had his hands pressed against his stomach and he was hunched over slightly, staring at Ramsey from the depths of his prominent brow.

Ramsey hadn't seen Victor's father since he was ten, but he remembered the man well enough to know that Victor looked just like him. Their mother referred to her ex-husband often as having been beaten hard with the ugly stick, and with the following breath would say that he and Victor could be twins.

Ramsey flitted his eyes around for the source of the clanging. It was easier than looking at the contorted, pained expression on his dead brother's face.

The wall above Victor's dresser was empty, where there had always been a mirror before. It must have fallen off the wall and disappeared behind the dresser, and that was the noise he had heard. Ramsey didn't need to investigate before he came to that conclusion. That was the thing about dreams.

*"I don't like you, but I love you..."* Victor sang softly underneath his breath, every word trembling as if they had to scrape their way out through his teeth. He held his gut and rocked back and forth while his eyes followed Ramsey, bloodshot to the point where the inflamed corners were angry, fire-rescue red. The song tapered off into a hum, which then ended in a flat, "You need to go, Ramsey."

"I didn't know that I was this tired," Ramsey told him, unable to keep his eyes off his brother's hands. Blood was starting to seep out from between Victor's woven fingers, bubbling every time he pressed them a little more into his stomach. "I feel like I can't wake up."

"That's the devil's doing." Victor winced, still rocking back and forth. "They want your creation."

Ramsey made a face. "You're not making sense," he said. Suddenly, there was a hard pull against his chest, like someone had wrapped a cord around his spine and was yanking on it. All the air expelled out of Ramsey's lungs at once and he couldn't draw in a new breath. Ramsey choked and gripped his own throat, digging his nails into his skin as if he could, somehow, puncture the windpipe for a savage tracheotomy.

Victor moaned and doubled over. More blood pumped from between his fingers, spreading down to his pants where a dark red stain bloomed over his thighs. "The longer I am here, the more I suffer. They *want* me to suffer." His dark brown eyes sparked. "You have to *fix it!*"

Ramsey wanted to say something like, '*as quickly as I can*', but he couldn't speak. All his words were just dust motes spinning around his brain, impossible to capture. Immense pressure piled up on his eyelids like two thumbs pushing down against his eyes, and the pressure kept building until wicked pain rocketed through his cranium.

The pain brought him back to his chair, to the living room, to consciousness. When he opened his eyes again, Ramsey was sitting up straight in his seat, looking into Adam's mismatched gaze that stared back at him with concern.

"Father?" The creature asked softly. It had a gentle voice, deeper than he thought it would be, but it was the dissonance of something with *that* face speaking so clearly and softly that made him recoil.

"Get back," Ramsey hissed, raising his hand as a warning. Adam looked deflated but pulled back away. It had already been crouched over his lap, and now it sat back on its heels with its long arms allowing its palms to bear its weight against the floor.

"You were..." The creature paused, as if wracking its brain for a word. "Twitching," it finally settled on.

The fact that it had accomplished so much linguistically in the time he had been asleep was miraculous, *astounding*, and Ramsey made a mental note to add a section in his journal. If only a few hours, if that, of being spoken and read to could kickstart the brain back into what it already knew, then what would days, maybe even weeks, of deliberate specialized education do?

"I was dreaming. Where is Abel?" Ramsey asked. The creature rocked a little on its heels.

"Kitchen," it finally said. Ramsey stood and turned around, and then he felt the creature grab him by the ankle.

"*Don't* touch me," Ramsey said sharply. Adam let go immediately, and there was some shuffling as it stood.

"Can I come with you?" the creature asked. "Scared to be...alone." It looked around while it asked.

"Absolutely absurd of you to be afraid," Ramsey said. "You're the most terrifying thing in this house."

"Me?" Adam placed a hand against its chest. A patch of skin above its crooked brow wrinkled.

"Yes, you," Ramsey said. "Have you seen yourself?" He grabbed the creature by the wrist and pulled it towards his mother's room. Adam stumbled behind him, unable to keep up with Ramsey's quick pace on account of how it was dragging the sides of its feet along the floorboards.

Ramsey half-dragged it all the way into his mother's bathroom and then positioned it in front of the mirror, grabbing its chin and pulling its head up so that it was staring at its own face straight-on. "That is what you look like," Ramsey said. "And that isn't usual. You know that, right? Look at me." He turned his own face towards the mirror. "What I am is whole. What you are is...parts."

Adam couldn't seem to tear its eyes away from its own reflection. It stood there, gripping the sides of the sink, its arms trembling as if it was exerting every ounce of effort it had to remain upright.

"That's not me," Adam said quietly. Ramsey turned to look at it again, studying its expression curiously.

"What do you mean, it isn't you?" Ramsey asked. That would be fascinating, if the brain had enough recollection to know what it 'should' look like, or in what ways it remembered the body it had been attached to previously.

Adam shook its head. "That's not me," it repeated. "I don't..." It raised one hand and touched the side of its face. Its rough fingers trailed along the silver stitches he'd created along the curve of its cheek. "...Was it you?"

"Of course, who else would it be?" Ramsey scoffed. "I put that face on you because the one you had was falling apart. Well, it was more complicated than that, but there's no explaining it to you."

Adam's gaze lingered on its reflection, but its tone took a sharp turn. "What did you do?"

Something about the sudden shift made Ramsey's gut twist. He took a step back, just enough to pull his own reflection out of the mirror's frame. "What do you mean? I gave you life," Ramsey said, matching the creature's tone to stand verbally toe-to-toe. "You wouldn't be standing here sounding so smart if it weren't for me. All the pieces of you would be rotting in different graves, along with that brain of yours." Ramsey rapped his knuckles against the side of Adam's skull, and the creature's hand shot up, seizing him by the wrist. It twisted around and used its grip to drag him closer until they were chest-to-chest, and Adam was staring down at him with that one green eye that was brighter than a lantern.

"*Don't.*" The way it spoke to him mimicked his own sharp commands too closely for his comfort. "That is *not nice.*"

"Nice?" Ramsey stared into its face, even though his heart was racing. "What do you know about nice, or kind, or right and wrong?"

Adam's expression shuttered and it let him go. Ramsey staggered back and watched the creature hunch over the sink, this time very deliberately not looking in the mirror.

"It's not my face," Adam repeated, its voice cracking. "It's wrong. Wrong and..." It dragged its hand down its face and didn't finish its sentence.

Ramsey could have sworn he saw a glistening trail resembling a tear race down its cheek and break apart on its thumb.

"Well," Ramsey said, recovering some of his dignity. "It was never meant to be yours, anyway."

The creature snapped its head towards him. "Who?" it demanded.

"That face was meant for my brother," Ramsey said. "So, it really doesn't matter whether you like it or not. You're stuck with it, because you stole it."

Adam growled. It balled its wide hands into fists and then slammed them against the sink. The porcelain cracked and a big piece went flying, shooting towards the bathtub. Ramsey's eyes widened and he took another step back, holding his hands out in a placating gesture.

"I did not *steal!*" Adam roared. Ramsey's eyebrows shot up.

"Adam." He pitched his voice low. "You need to calm down."

Adam shook its head. "I don't know...how." It slammed its hands against the broken sink bowl again. One hair's breadth over to the left and it would have sliced open its whole hand. "I don't know...and it hurts." It drew its hand close to its chest and pounded the center.

"You just need to breathe," Ramsey said. "In through your nose. Out through your mouth." He demonstrated a few times, waving his hand in encouragement to try and get the creature to mimic him. Adam swayed on its feet but couldn't seem to get the hang of what he was trying to tell it. If Adam went down, Ramsey might consider it for the best, as long as the creature didn't bust its skull open on the way to the floor.

"There you are," Abel's voice floated over, and suddenly Ramsey's mild panic was replaced by irritation. "You got away from me."

The creature whimpered and then whipped around, grabbing Abel's arms and burying its face in their shoulder. Abel rested their hands against Adam's back, patting it gently and cradling the creature like a mother with her child.

Ramsey thought about commenting on the display, but he bit his tongue instead. "Adam broke the sink," he said. "If you're staying here tonight, then you will have to use the other bathroom."

"That is all right," Abel said, and flashed a smile. "Are you asking me to stay the night?"

"It isn't much of a request," Ramsey said flatly. He liked to think that they were both very aware of the situation, enough that Abel shouldn't have to ask why Ramsey was not ready to let them waltz out his front door.

"Well, I am flattered." Abel ran their hand down Adam's long hair before detaching themselves, gently. "Do you mind sharing?" They cupped the creature's face as they asked.

Adam furrowed its brow and shook its head. "Why?" it asked.

"Not everyone likes to share." Abel flicked their Autumn-brown eyes back towards Ramsey. "So, I always ask."

Ramsey rolled his eyes. He moved past the two of them, with Abel stepping back to clear the way, and didn't feel like he could breathe again until he was standing in an open space.

"If Adam stays with me, does he have to be restrained?" Abel asked.

"Just lock the door," Ramsey said. "I don't give a damn what you do."

# CHAPTER ELEVEN

Ramsey took another shower before crawling into bed. This time, his clothes were clean, but he wasn't nearly as tired as he felt he should be. He chalked it up to the nap he had taken in the middle of the day, which had clearly been a mistake.

There was so much he *could* have been doing, but instead he was laying in bed, watching his fan spin and turning over half a dozen different thoughts. He still hadn't shaken the eerie feeling that stuck with him from his dream, and it was stranger still that Wisp had been silent for the rest of the day. Of course, Ramsey was used to periods of inactivity, where Wisp would go dormant and then resurface days later with more than enough racket to make up for the quiet. But the timing was *odd*. And he couldn't get Victor's expression out of his head.

*'The devil wants your creation.'* What did that even mean?

Ramsey rolled over onto his side to stare at the wall. His back hurt too much for him to stay flat. In the darkness, his eyes played tricks, creating little blots of color that twisted and writhed and made it look as though something was moving where there was nothing. He needed to get up. He needed to *do* something. To catalog his findings, to go out searching for more bodies and parts to get started on his next great work. In the Bible, God only took one day to rest. For Ramsey, it already felt like he had been laying around for three. Like somehow, he had missed an entire week, and it had been that long since he had touched his tools.

*'Life without work.'* Was it even worth living?

Something moved at the end of the bed, brushing against his foot. Ramsey sat up immediately and jerked his leg up, grabbing the covers and flinging them off. It wasn't so completely dark that he couldn't make out the banana-yellow coloring of a curled-up snake against his white sheets.

Ramsey jumped out of bed, nearly falling when he landed on his bad leg and his knee almost gave out underneath him. He kept his eyes on the snake while looking for something to throw on top of it, or hit it with—that would actually let him grab hold the thing without getting bitten. His toes collided with one of his boots, and Ramsey bent down to pick it up, because it was at least a *start*.

He only took his eyes off the snake for a second. When he looked again, it was gone. His heart jumped into his throat and he pulled the covers off the bed all the way, dragging them towards him and searching the floor.

A soft laugh brushed against his ear, and Ramsey flung the boot into a dark corner. It hit the wall with a *thump*.

"Man of science," Abel's voice broke through the quiet. "What scared you now?"

"There's a snake in here, watch where you step." Ramsey said. He hadn't heard the door open, and he was pretty sure he had locked it anyway. But he was less concerned about the intrusion than he was the possibility of getting bitten.

"Is that so? I didn't see it," Abel said. "Are you sure you did not dream it?"

"Yes," Ramsey said. He took his eyes off the floor long enough to glare. Abel sat on the foot on the bed, wearing a long, patterned nightgown that had belonged to his mother. Their wavy brown hair tumbled down their back, with only a few out-of-place strands framing their face.

Seeing his mother's nightgown on the body of what was less of a stranger, more of an intruder at this point, made Ramsey clench his jaw so hard his teeth hurt. And for half a second, he forgot all about the snake.

"You really should ask for permission," Ramsey said, "before you just take things from a dead woman's closet."

"Oh, forgive me. I didn't think she'd mind." Abel kept their bare feet on the floor, clearly unconcerned, and twisted their long fingers up into the nightgown's skirt. "I'll take it off."

Ramsey scoffed overtly. "You're wearing it now; you might as well keep it on."

"There's logic, for you." Abel transferred their busy fingers to their hair. "You're up very late, doctor. I would have thought you'd be gone from exhaustion."

"I'm not as tired as I should be," he admitted. He took another step back, still looking for the snake. Although the longer he went without spotting it again, the more he was convinced that maybe he *had* imagined it.

"Then I am surprised you are still in bed," Abel said conversationally. "I would think that a busy mind like yours would be unable to stop itself from moving on to the next project."

Ramsey paused. "I should be working," he admitted. Of course, he had been grappling with that notion for hours, but now that it was coming out of Abel's mouth, repeating it aloud felt like closure.

"I didn't say that," Abel reprimanded him gently. "It was more of an observation. You're very twitchy."

"Twitchy?" Ramsey bundled his bedcover back up and dropped it onto the bed. "No, I'm not."

"Restless, is that what you prefer?" Abel tilted their head. "You are always working as if you are not guaranteed to see the sunrise."

"I'm not," Ramsey said. "No one is."

"Of course not," Abel allowed. "You know that well, being surrounded by death for your entire career." They shifted, turning their body more towards him while pulling up one leg to tuck underneath the nightgown's hem. "Do you do anything else, Doctor Abernathy?"

"Anything else?" Ramsey echoed. "Like what?"

"Is it always dead bodies?" Abel asked. "Is it ever living flesh?" Their fingers continued to twist through long strands of their hair as they spoke. "Do you entertain yourself with reading, or with art?"

"No," Ramsey said. He didn't mean to sound so disgusted, but the idea of stepping away from his work in order to engage with something that didn't *matter* at all made him itch. "No, there was time for that once, but not anymore. When I was a kid, I used to read. Catch frogs with my brother, that sort of thing."

"That is sad," Abel said. There was no ridicule in their voice, only soft, gentle pity. Ramsey *hated* that intonation. If there was one thing he never wanted from another living soul, it was pity, especially when his situation was far from a piteous one.

"Is it?" he snapped. "I think you have forgotten who you are speaking with—what I have discovered and *created* here."

"Is it good to anyone?" Abel spread their hands. "Is it any good to *you?*"

Ramsey's nostrils flared. "The gift of life? Is that any good? Overcoming death, does that have no benefit?" Ramsey put his knee on the bed and grabbed Abel by the shoulders. "You don't understand anything, or you are goading me. I'm not sure what the answer is. You praised my work earlier. Were you lying to me because you were afraid of having your jaw dislocated?"

"No, darling. I'm not afraid of you." Abel's shoulder moved against his hand as they raised

117

their own and brought their fingers to rest against his cheek. Their fingers were cool against his blazing-hot skin. Ramsey hadn't even realized how hot he was until they touched him. "And I don't think you would dislocate my jaw."

"Then you're mistaken," Ramsey said. "Because I was going to."

"Were you?" Abel tapped his cheek pensively. "You could try, I suppose."

"Try to, what? Overpower you? That isn't hard." Ramsey let out a fast breath. "I've already got you at a disadvantage."

"Oh, yes?" Abel smiled again. "Because you have your hands on my shoulders?"

"I am much broader than you," Ramsey pointed out.

"Yes, and weaker, too." At that, Abel wrapped one of their legs around Ramsey's hips and pulled him down. They turned one of their shoulders at the same time and used the leverage to flip him over onto his back. Ramsey found himself staring up at the ceiling at an odd angle with Abel straddling his hips like he was a show pony.

"It's because your legs and back are weak," they said. "Don't think I didn't notice."

Ramsey grabbed hold of their thighs, intent on flinging them off. "You need to get back to your room," he said, too disgruntled to counter their point. "Before that creature wakes up and starts crying because it can't find you."

A frown touched Abel's lips, but it didn't stay. They settled against his hips so that he could feel their heat through the thin fabric of his bed pants, and how stiff they were.

"You're awful, Doctor Abernathy," Abel said. They leaned over his chest and slipped their hands underneath his shirt. Their cool fingers slid over his ribs and up his pectorals, grabbing his chest and squeezing his nipples like they couldn't help themselves.

Ramsey grabbed hold of their ass and hauled them up a little higher, until the only thing between his cock and their back entrance was two folds of cotton. "I'm not sure about being an awful man," he said. "But I am an honest one."

"Honest with who?" They let out a sharp laugh. Abel pulled the nightgown up and reached down to brush their fingers over the crotch of his pants. They reached through the front and took hold of his cock, stroking it just a few times before pulling it through so that it stood up straight with its throbbing head pressed against their inner thigh.

"If you want someone to fuck you," Ramsey said, his throat tight, "you need to get better at not laughing in their face."

"You are plenty turned on without me molly-coddling your ego, doctor," Abel said. "Anymore than I have been, at least." They lowered themselves until their body rested against his, chest-to-chest, and rubbed their own slender, long cock against his thicker one. "How long has it been since you let that busy mind of yours rest?"

Too long, but Ramsey didn't want to dwell on it. If he let his thoughts get away from him then he would be thinking about Adam and Wisp, and all the other hungry, demanding little tasks that commanded his every waking moment. Ramsey brought his knee up and braced himself to try and flip Abel over, but they put a stop to that by pinning his thigh down and sinking their teeth into his neck.

Ramsey exclaimed loudly and Abel purred, kissing his jaw as if to apologize and then drawing their hips up so that they could rest the tip of his cock against their ass. They dragged their hand along his neck and their fingers came back a little bloody. Ramsey didn't think that they had bitten him hard enough to break the skin, but there it was.

Abel touched his cock with their bloody hand, squeezing gently and stroking along the foreskin until Ramsey felt like he was going to burst from their touch alone. His cock quivered in their hands and they angled it just right, sliding down the shaft with their tight, *tight* ring of muscle fighting against every inch.

Ramsey moaned, rolling his hips to thrust while keeping them close at the same time. He loved the feeling of their chest pressed against his, and his only wish was that they were naked. He groped their narrow waist through the loose nightgown, moving his hands up and down their sharp hips and their round, tight ass. Abel eventually pulled themselves up, gyrating their hips to ride him even harder, moving up and down his length with such ferocity that Ramsey's ability to think flew completely out the window.

It had been too long. He was going to cum. Abel slipped the nightgown off and tossed it onto the bed, and Ramsey saw their cock sticking up like a mast, perfectly flushed and beautiful, leaking pre-cum that dripped down the front and covered their fingers while they stoked themselves. Ramsey touched every part of them that he could reach, lost in their skin and in the way they made him feel completely used, like he could have been anything they wanted to ride in order to get themselves off. There was something about that realization, too, that drove him wild. To be an object, to be almost *disregarded*...it was so good that he, almost, didn't want to be allowed to orgasm at all.

Something brushed against his shoulder, and Ramsey ignored it. But then he felt it slide across his throat, and he caught a glimpse of bright yellow in his peripheral vision. *That goddamn snake!*

"Fuck!" Ramsey tried to sit up. Abel slammed their hands against his chest and kept him down on the bed, hips still undulating with all their long brown hair falling around their shoulders.

"Giving up on me?" they asked, grinning.

"There's a snake!" Ramsey tried to push them off again, and Abel doubled down, grinding on his cock and rocking back and forth until he felt like it was going to snap in half.

"Doctor Abernathy, man of science, you're so afraid of everything," they laughed breathlessly. "There's nothing there."

"Fuck if there isn't!" Ramsey gathered up all his strength and pushed them off. Abel fell onto the bed and Ramsey slammed his hand across their face. It happened too quickly for him to even try and stop it, and the sound of his knuckles colliding with their flesh brought a deafening silence in its wake.

But it was satisfying, bringing as much relief as an orgasm, so he did it again.

The second time he hit them, a stream of cum slipped out of Ramsey's half-erect cock.

Abel did not move. They regarded him, stonily, while a pink mark blossomed on their cheek from where his hand had landed—twice.

Ramsey swallowed hard and pushed his cock back into his pants.

"I think you should go to bed," Ramsey said. He picked up the nightgown from where it had fallen on the bed and threw it towards them. He took a step back to give them some room, and his foot landed on top of something that twisted underneath it. Something sank into his foot, what stung like a needle, and he dropped down to one knee, hissing through his teeth while trying not to scream from pain.

A yellow tail disappeared underneath his bed.

"See where fear gets you?" Abel stepped off the bed, clothed once more, and reached underneath it. They pulled the snake out as easily as if it were a stuffed animal and held it up for Ramsey to see. "I don't think it's venomous, but you're the doctor."

Ramsey's entire foot throbbed. The pain eclipsed any quip he might have, and all he could say was, "get out."

Abel shrugged. They lifted the snake towards their shoulders and allowed it to slide around their neck before they left the room.

# CHAPTER TWELVE

The next morning, Ramsey's eggs were burned, and his toast looked more like two black charcoal briquettes stacked on top of one another. Abel's gentle and mild demeanor, by contrast, had not changed one ounce.

Which, Ramsey had reasoned, was likely only because Adam was in the room.

Turning his attention to his creature was a lot easier than lingering over the events of the night before. Ramsey's foot was bruised where the snake had bit him, but there was minimal swelling and the pain was not bad enough to make him consider going to a hospital. Before leaving his bedroom, he had dug the Percocet prescription bottle out of his laundry pile and popped one of the remaining pills. The world was a little fuzzy, but it made focusing on Adam easy.

His creature looked up at him from across the table. Adam had only been prodding at its food until Abel sat down, and then it started eating voraciously.

Ramsey sipped on the coffee he'd made himself.

"Father," the creature said. Ramsey interjected by snapping his fingers before he could finish swallowing.

"I am not your father," he said when he could finally speak. "It is *doctor*."

The creature didn't miss a beat. "You're hurt." It tapped two fingers against the side of its neck, indicating the place on Ramsey's where he had been bitten. The shallow wound had already scabbed over and was wreathed by an ugly bruise. Ramsey's neck was sore, but otherwise it didn't really hurt and he had almost forgotten about it.

"I was bitten by a snake," he said, sipping at his coffee again.

Abel smirked and lit a cigarette.

"I have some work to do in the front yard," Ramsey said. "I haven't checked on it since that storm, and I'm sure it needs cleaning up."

"I'm sure it does," Abel said mildly. "Adam and I will keep each other company. Don't worry."

"We are almost done with our first book," Adam said quietly. Although its vocabulary was growing, it was pitching its voice lower and softer than before, as if it was losing confidence with every pulse of electricity that woke up a new segment of its brain.

"Who knows what other useful skills Abel can teach you?" Ramsey said, only half-sarcastically. "I imagine by the end of the week you will be able to count to ten."

Adam pressed its lips together and looked back down at its plate. It pushed a mound of scrambled egg towards the edge, sullenly, but Ramsey was not concerned with its pouting.

The front of the house was a mess. Ramsey spent a few hours just clearing branches and storm debris, which wouldn't have taken so long if he wasn't dragging along the leg he had hurt from climbing the fence. He vowed to check the wound after his next shower to make sure it was healing and that there was no infection setting in. He realized that he should have been more concerned, but it was hardly a priority with so many other things that needed his attention.

Ramsey checked on his boat, making sure it was still tied to the dock and that no fallen branches had inflicted any damage. He picked up an overturned paint bucket and something rolled out from underneath, covered in dirt and leaf litter, enormous and white like a giant mushroom.

Ramsey nudged it with his foot, pushing whatever it was towards the bank. The round white thing rolled, and when he caught a glimpse of what looked like a human face. Ramsey nearly dropped the paint bucket as he knelt down to investigate. He wasn't wearing gloves, so his fingers sank into the sides of whatever-it-was, and the spongy texture made his stomach flip. But it was a face, all right—a face attached to a whole human head. It was as round and bald as an egg, and it looked so familiar. Ramsey wracked his brain, trying to place where he had seen it before. But it hadn't been the head under the cypress tree, he had taken that off and used it for Adam...

*The graveyard.* That was it. He was holding the exact head that he had severed from the torso he had gleaned for Adam's form. Ramsey gripped it tight, staring down at its sunken sockets, his hand shaking even though—logistically—it made perfect sense. The grave

had no doubt flooded and the head would have been one of many body parts to get swept away by the current. It happened all the time. That was how most of them ended up in his yard to begin with.

Even as he considered the

logical circumstances, he couldn't bring himself to drop the head.

And then the eyelids moved.

At first, he wasn't sure of what he had seen, but then they twitched again, and the second time it was unmistakable. The eyelids were glued down in typical undertaker fashion, but their thin skin bulged like there was a finger behind them, prodding to get out.

Ramsey stood up, still holding the head. He watched the eyes with morbid fascination, wondering if it was some sort of parasite or even a twitch from some of the left-behind nerves. Then one of the eyelids sprang open, and a pointed yellow head with dark, beady eyes slid out from the mangled socket. A long, yellow snake came sliding out, regarding him only briefly before turning and diving into the narrow space between the slack lips. A horrified chill ran up Ramsey's spine and he dropped the head, slamming his foot into it and sending it sailing across the yard. The head spun through the air and landed straight into the water, where it sank unceremoniously, snake and all.

That was the second, no, the *third* snake he had seen with that coloring—and he still had no idea what it was. Ramsey's heart pounded thunderously behind his ribs and he rubbed his sternum to try and calm himself down. He picked up the paint bucket and dropped it on his porch on his way back up. He didn't even realize until he hit his door that his hands were shaking.

"Adam," he rasped as soon as he was inside the house. "I am going to make coffee." The act of speaking aloud was grounding. It didn't really matter to him whether he got a response. Ramsey glanced towards the living room as he passed it, his heart still hammering in a way that was making his forehead clammy.

A loud groan came from the living room, and when Ramsey looked in, he saw Abel spread out on the low coffee table, holding Adam's head between their legs. The creature was kneeling between their thighs, its head bobbing up and down their long, slender cock. Abel's fingers were tangled in its wild, dark hair, and their legs were wrapped around its shoulders, heels resting against its back.

Abel turned their head and looked Ramsey in the eye, their expression one of more snide satisfaction than perfect ecstasy. That did not stop them, however, from moaning again and making a series of quick, breathy sounds as though they were on the edge of climax.

Abel's plush mouth formed an orgasmic 'O', and Ramsey could have sworn he saw the snake's yellow head peaking out of their mouth, just as it had with the dismembered head in the yard.

Ramsey blazed into the living room and grabbed Adam by the hair. Blood rushing angrily to his face, heart beating a hundred miles a minute until he thought he was going to have a heart attack.

"What the hell do you think you are doing?" Ramsey snarled. "Under my roof?"

Adam yelled wordlessly and reached up, wrapping its fingers around his in an attempt to pry him loose. When the red cleared from Ramsey's vision, he noticed Abel sitting cross-legged on the floor across the table, glasses perched on the bridge of their nose and fully clothed.

"What's wrong?" Abel asked. They had their fingers splayed across the pages of a book, the middle two resting against the dark, deep crease.

Ramsey swallowed. He let go of Adam's hair. "I saw..." He took a deep breath. "Another snake." *'I don't think you are what you say that you are,'* is what he wanted to say. And Wisp's warning of the word *'devil'* was now circulating through his brain.

Ramsey had assumed that Wisp was assigning the derogatory term to *him,* but maybe it was more literal than that.

"The same one, do you think?" Abel asked. They reached across the table and touched

Adam's hand, stroking their thumb over the creature's large knuckles.

"No," Ramsey said. "Or, really, I don't know."

"Snakes aren't dangerous," Adam muttered. Abel smiled at that.

"Not generally," they agreed. "Only when provoked, most of the time. And even then, only the venomous kind."

"I am going to bring my shovel inside," Ramsey said, itching his nose. "If I see it again, I'm going to take off its head."

"No!" Adam protested.

"The only good snake is a dead one." Ramsey looked over at Abel. "At least when it's caught in the house."

Abel adjusted their glasses and turned another page in their book. "We are on the last chapter," they said. "Would you like to sit down and listen?"

"No." Ramsey shook his head and stepped away. "I am going to make my coffee. Then I'm going to grab my shovel and hunt for that snake."

"Suit yourself," Abel said. They lowered their lashes and gazed up at Ramsey through them. "Adam is such *fulfilling* company."

In that moment, Ramsey wanted to rip the stitches out of Adam's neck and tear off that head he had so carefully placed. He wanted to stomp on the resurrected skull until it broke apart and then sweep the pieces outside and into the swamp. What he had seen still flashed across his mind's eye, and it was the unmitigated *gall* of Abel's tone that implied Adam could do something, *anything* that Ramsey couldn't.

Even though none of the vision had been real, and Abel couldn't see inside his mind, Ramsey felt that they somehow *knew* what he had seen. Furthermore, they had somehow *orchestrated* it. He didn't know how, but he had a feeling that Adam knew, too.

A waste. Both of them. Better off dead and reduced to parts than *this*. Better off made into something else.

While Ramsey brewed his coffee, he set his journal on the counter and sketched out a new figure. He circled all the parts that were hardest to come by and squiggled the word 'Abel?' on a line next to each one.

The biggest exception was the head. He circled that and wrote 'Adam' right next to it, then drew another line coming from the dead eye where he wrote '*replace*'.

After all, if he was going to do it all again, he might as well do it right.

# Chapter Thirteen

After an hour of searching his yard for the snake, prodding clusters of long grass and striking roots with the head of his shovel, Ramsey decided to give up for the day. After dinner, he lingered at the kitchen table with the shovel propped up in a corner behind him, while he worked on his notes about the miraculous development of Adam's transformation—although the results of his continued experiment were the farthest thing on his mind. All he *really* wanted to focus on was the new creature he had to build, the one that would finally give Wisp the body that they wanted—the body that *Victor* deserved. The only light came from a yellow bulb above the kitchen sink. Every other part of the house was pitch-black.

Shuffling. Ramsey looked up to see Adam's lumbering form shuffle into view. The creature's hair had been combed and was pulled back away from its face, and even though it was still wearing the same wrinkled clothes Ramsey had dressed it in, it looked almost handsome.

Ramsey attributed that to the low lighting.

"Doctor," Adam greeted him. Ramsey acknowledged it with a nod.

"I thought you were in bed," Ramsey said. The creature pulled out a chair from across the table and sat down.

"I was," it said. "I couldn't sleep." It looked him up and down, as if just now seeing him for the first time. Ramsey allowed the quiet scrutiny, returning it in kind. His creature, his monster, his beautiful creation was nearly passable as a man. If it weren't for the knotted scar tissue forming in the seams along its face, it would have been impeccable.

Because, somehow, the previously dead and wrinkled skin was filling out. It was no longer the color of a dead fish' underbelly, but the colors that elected to return were more mismatched than before. And that single green eye more than made up for its twin, where being caught in its line of sight was like being thrown in the path of a boat light.

It was an invaluable observation. While Ramsey hated that he would have to detach the head again, he at least had an idea of what Victor would look like once his blood started pumping and his neurons began firing.

"I'm not what you wanted," the creature said. "I know that. You've told me."

"You were meant to be my brother," Ramsey replied. "But you took on a life of your own. And now he is still lingering, and waiting, and I have to take care of you."

The creature winced a little but did not respond to the jab. "This body isn't mine," it changed the subject. "Is there any part of me...that was attached before?" It sounded like it was struggling to form the question it was trying to ask. Ramsey had enough of an idea that he responded.

"I don't think so," he said. "Your brain was more than likely one of the first things I collected, and the rest of you came much later. So maybe there is a kidney somewhere in there, or a twist of intestine that was original to your system. But most everything else was harvested along the way." He tried to conjure up an analogy and failed. It didn't matter, anyway. "Everything you have now is *better*. I made sure to take only the best of what I could find."

"Better..." Adam seemed to have a hard time swallowing that. It looked down at its hands and picked at the edges of its fingernails. "I was supposed to be perfect, but I am a mistake."

"I don't make mistakes," Ramsey cut in. "If you are imperfect, it is caused by factors outside of my control. I cannot dig into your brain and change your personality, as much as I would like to."

Adam was quiet again for a full minute, then it nodded. "And you want me to go," it said at last.

"No, absolutely not. I want you to stay." Ramsey said. "Even imperfect, you are still a marvel to be studied. I have a lot to learn from you, and in learning I will duplicate the method without so many variables. My brother will have his body, and then everything will be as it should."

"I see." Adam licked its dry, dark lips. "What was your brother...like?"

"Victor?" Ramsey looked down at his notes. All the scribbled, impossible handwriting scrunched together and looked more like ants marching across the page than legible words. "He was a kid when he died. He was just old enough to drink—I know that doesn't mean anything to you." He swept his hand over his face. "Or maybe it does. There was ten years between us, so I didn't know him as well as I could have."

"Is that why you want him back?" the creature asked. Ramsey shook his head.

"I have no choice but to bring him back," he said. "If I don't, then he will never rest. He is already always asking, *demanding*—you should have heard the tantrum he threw when he could not settle into..." He gestured. "You."

"You don't want him, then." The creature gazed past Ramsey's shoulder, seemingly lost in thought—although Ramsey wasn't sure just how many thoughts could be circulating through that head. "You don't want anyone."

Ramsey rolled his eyes. "It isn't that simple," he said. "Not that I would expect you to understand why."

"I understand more now," Adam said a bit testily for the first time. "More than you think. And I talk to Abel, who explains things to me."

The mention of Abel cut Ramsey's patience for the conversation in half. "Abel doesn't know anything," Ramsey said shortly. "They only want you to think that they do, because they are trying to make you rely on them."

"Why would they do that?" Adam asked.

"Because if you rely on them, then you will want to stay with them," Ramsey said. "And if they ever leave, you will want to go with them, which I will not allow. They want you to think that I am being unfair, so that you resent me, and try to leave. They want us to fight."

Adam crinkled its brow and shook its head. "I don't think that they want that," it said. "I just think that they are a very...kind."

"And that is exactly why you *cannot* leave," Ramsey scoffed. "You could never tell whether someone was being truly kind or not. You don't have the discernment to understand someone else's hidden motives. People are never *just* kind, and Abel is certainly not without their agenda."

Adam expanded its chest with a deep breath before exhaling through its nose. "When your brother comes," it said, "what will happen to me?"

"I don't figure that you will have much to worry about," Ramsey said dismissively, turning back to his notes. "Go back to bed."

The creature lingered at the table for a moment before pushing its chair back and rising. It looked like it wanted to say something else, but its face quickly disappeared into shadow when it drew itself up to its full height. "Can we talk more, later?" it asked.

"If you can think of different questions, I will answer them," Ramsey said. He flicked his pen dismissively. "Get on, now."

The creature obeyed, turning around and taking heavy steps back towards the bedroom.

# CHAPTER FOURTEEN

Smoke curled from the end of Abel's lit cigarette and streamed from between their pillowy lips. They sat on the back porch with their face turned towards the rising sun, where the breaking dawn left brushstrokes of crimson and gold over their celestial features. Ramsey watched them with his hand wrapped around the glass neck of a ginger beer, his free arm resting against the side of the house and bearing all his weight.

"Did you ever find your snake?" Abel asked. They turned their head to face him, and for half a moment their brown eyes flashed red.

Ramsey took another sip of ginger beer and shook his head. "Wasted my time just by looking," he said. "Damn thing's the least of my worries out here."

Abel played their lips over the end of the cigarette holder. "I will have to leave, eventually," they said, their tone deceptively demure.

"Eventually," Ramsey said. He wasn't going to argue with that, although the circumstances under which they might be allowed to leave were very much up for debate.

"Adam will want to come with me," Abel continued. "You know that he will."

"It doesn't matter what Adam wants." Ramsey took another swig and paused to let the carbonation settle on his tongue. "It is a beautiful creation, but it does not have human rights. The pieces that it's made of might not all even have the *same* rights. And its place is here, with me. I don't think you're naïve enough to really think it stands a snowball's chance in hell outside of these walls."

"Is that what you will tell him?" Abel asked. "A snowball's chance? He already thinks that you hate him."

Ramsey sucked on his teeth. "That's stupid. And however *it* feels about me, I'm sure those feelings are only exacerbated by whatever narrative you happen to be feeding it."

Abel's gaze slid up and down Ramsey's form again, taking him in slowly as if searching for something. "You really think so?" They let loose another stream of smoke. "All right, Doctor Abernathy. I'll bite. Is *anything* your fault?"

"There is no fault to be found, here," Ramsey said, pushing himself away from the wall. "You are seeking answers to a problem that does not exist. When the truth is that you are the one who came into my home uninvited, and you have made yourself increasingly unwelcome since."

"I came to you in need and have since become a prisoner, more or less by your own admission." They held up a hand. "It is a pattern I have noticed with you, so don't worry. I don't think any higher of myself for it."

"Nothing here is a prisoner. Or, if there is one at all, it is me," Ramsey said. "I could not walk out that door if I tried. I would be dragged back by a wailing ghost or that whimpering creature, chained down by expectations and demands that often exceed what I am capable of. And yet, do I not work to conquer my own

143

shortcomings? What choice have I had, *except* to work?"

Abel considered the smoldering end of their cigarette. "When you write a book, what will it be called?" they asked. Ramsey took a moment to blink and digest the question, thrown off course by their tangent.

"*Creator,*" he said.

Abel nodded. "How badly do you want to take that bottle, smash it, and jam the pieces into my throat?"

The answer was pulled out of him by an invisible line. "Badly," he admitted.

Abel smiled. "You have so much anger," they said. "A lot of men do, so I'm not very surprised. But you admit it to yourself, and I think that's swell." They teased the end of their cigarette holder with their tongue before taking another drag, sucking the cigarette down to its filter. "Just be careful with Adam. He's not as fragile as you think."

Ramsey shot them a look. Something about the way they phrased things put his hackles up. "We're not talking about you leaving," he warned.

"Not talking about nothing, darlin'." Abel pitched their cigarette butt over the porch railing and then stood up. "I think I've been away from home long enough." They were wearing the same clothes they arrived in, except this time their hair was in two braids that started at their crown and draped down their back like lengths of rope.

Panic kicked up in Ramsey's chest. He grabbed Abel's arm as they walked past, certain that they did not understand just how gravely serious he was regarding their situation.

"You've seen Adam," he said. "You know what lives here. And you are going to just go on, and not bring every wheedling journalist and blood-sucking government leech to my door?"

"Why would I do that?" Abel asked. They took their arm back, slipping right through his grasp. Ramsey watched them walk away for half a second before following them inside.

"Why would you?" Ramsey snapped. "Because you want Adam for yourself. Mm!" He slammed his mostly-empty bottle down on the counter as he passed. "I know that!"

"Who told you that?" Abel kept walking, although they didn't seem to be in any hurry. They made a beeline for the front door and Adam, who was sitting in the living room, stood up as soon as it saw them pass the entrance.

"Abel?" For just a moment, the creature sounded lost. "Where are you going?"

"I am sorry, beloved." Abel stopped long enough to cup Adam's face in their hands. "I have to return home, I cannot live here. Your father doesn't want me to." They smiled.

"Besides, you don't need me anymore. You've picked up everything so quickly."

"Wait!" Adam caught Abel's wrists, its gentle voice pitched higher than usual with panic. "I don't want you to leave." It held their gaze. "Stay with me, please."

"No, love—but I will do my best to visit you soon," Abel crooned. While the two made their pitiful exchange, Ramsey grabbed his shovel from the corner where he had left it propped up. He gripped the thick handle in both fists, but the way his bad knee wobbled made him almost wish he had grabbed his cane, instead.

"Father..." Adam turned its mismatched gaze on Ramsey, who clutched the shovel handle even tighter. "Don't make—"

"I am *not* your father!" Ramsey barked. Adam flinched, but did not shrink back fully, still holding Abel's wrists.

"Ramsey is a doctor," Abel said, not the least bit visibly fazed by the presence of the shovel. "He was only ever taught to wash his hands of things, and nothing else."

"I was taught," Ramsey seethed, "to *fix* things. What they neglected to emphasize was how *thankless* a job it is."

Abel's smile was thin as they walked out the front door. Adam stumbled after them, reaching for their arm, too panicked to even walk straight on ungainly legs that had not yet regained their full strength. Ramsey charged past his creature, gripping the shovel with both hands and flipping it around so that the head was in the air. Abel made it only as far as the top of the stairs before Ramsey brought the shovel down, swinging it through the air, the motion ending with the edge biting deep into the back of their skull.

The sound of metal colliding with bone was followed by awful silence. Adam stood at the top of the stairs only a few inches away from where Abel was completely frozen, staring at the back of their head as if it could not quite comprehend what it was seeing. After a split second, Ramsey regained his momentum and yanked the shovel back. Blood spurted from the ugly head wound and splattered across Adam's face, which seemed to send it into a frenzy from the way it started screaming.

The sound that came out of Adam's mouth sounded like a dying fox. Abel's body tilted forward and then tumbled down the stairs, bouncing off the shallow wooden steps until it landed with a heavy *thunk* against the damp ground. Ramsey wasn't far behind. When he reached the bottom of the steps, he ground his foot against Abel's back, pushing their face down into the mud before he raised his shovel again and drove the tip down towards their neck. He struck them twice, and the second blow almost severed their head completely.

Ramsey was not able to step back and examine his work before Adam barreled into him. The creature shoved him to the ground and Ramsey raised the shovel in his own defense, locking the thick wooden handle between them as they both grabbed on. There was something in Adam's face he had never seen before, a vicious, *furious* expression contorted by its pathetic howls.

Ramsey brought up his knee and dug it into Adam's chest. He pushed against the shovel and threw the creature off him, buying just enough time to pull himself up to his feet. He raised the shovel high and turned its side outward, threatening Adam with the bloody edge.

"I do *not* want to drop you right here," Ramsey warned. "But I will. Stand *down*."

Adam reeled back. It stood there, feet half-buried in the mud, with its hands forming claws at its sides while its chest heaved over several hard-won breaths. Several sections of its curly black hair had fallen into its face and it glared at Ramsey through the strands. In all his life, Ramsey had never seen so much hate directed so pointedly towards him.

"They were not what they seemed," Ramsey said, trying his best to recover control of the situation.

"You killed them," Adam breathed, and every word sounded pained. "Are you going to fix it?"

*'Fix it'* echoed through Ramsey's head. The sound of Wisp's voice accompanied by a dozen cups raining from the cupboards to the kitchen floor. But this was not Wisp. This was not something he *needed* to fix.

Not in the way that Adam wanted him to, at any rate. There was plenty to be done, and nothing would go to waste.

"It is not that simple." Feeling more confident in himself, Ramsey stepped closer to Adam, still gripping the shovel. "Do you think that I can accomplish what I did for you anytime that I want? That is not how these things are done..." His words trailed off when he glanced back towards the stairs.

Abel's body was completely gone, severed head and all. Ramsey's face must have gone visibly white, because Adam asked, "What?" and turned around as well.

The creature stared at the empty place, as confused as its creator, if not more so. Ramsey set the tip of his shovel against the ground and raked a hand through his hair, trying to gather his thoughts.

A body in that state couldn't just get up and walk away. Abel was for sure, without a doubt, dead. Ramsey had killed them. Earlier than he intended to, and more brutally than was necessary, but he *had* done it.

And now, they were just gone.

*'My house was broken into, and now it's full of water'* were some of the first words that Abel had said to him. Ramsey thought about the head that had washed up onto the bank—the same head that had floated out of a coffin he had broken into, a coffin covered in strange markings that had doubtlessly been filled with water from the hurricane. *'The devil',* Wisp kept saying. *'The devil wants your creation.'*

"Where are they?" Adam asked. That simple, stupid question brought Ramsey back to reality.

"A gator got them," Ramsey said with as much decisive authority as he could muster. "Gators are lightning-quick, and they can grab things when you're not looking. Get inside." He gestured up the stairs.

Adam looked around, almost like it didn't believe him, but then it started up the stairs. Ramsey followed it, concentrating on taking one deep, even breath after another. His spiraling thoughts were another matter.

"This is bad," Ramsey said, once the door was shut and locked behind them. "Worse than I could have thought."

"What do you mean?" Adam asked.

"Well, a gator won't eat the whole thing," Ramsey said. "So, some of that body is going to wash up onto a different bank. Someone is going to stumble across it, and who do you think they are going to come after?"

"Who?" Adam's eyes went round. "You?"

"No," Ramsey snapped. "*You*. They are going to take one look at you and they won't wait for an explanation. You look like you could rip someone's head off easily. They'll be dozens of people who will have you in pieces at the bottom of the swamp before you can blink. And if they come after you, then I am not going to be able to stop them. I'm not strong enough."

Adam shrank into itself. Ramsey's heart finally slowed back to its normal pace. At least *this* was falling back into his control. Something he could deal with.

"I didn't hurt them," Adam said. It dragged its fingers down through its hair, pulling even more of the strands loose from its tie.

"I know that," Ramsey said. "But no one will understand that, and they won't try. So, we have to stay here and keep to ourselves. If a few days go by, and no one comes, then we know we are in the clear."

A few days would be enough for him to gather up new materials. If he could just keep Adam inside the house, then he could try again with a new creation for his brother—and then he would not have to deal with this any longer.

Adam was quaking. A tear slipped down its cheek, followed immediately by two more, and Ramsey could not help but be impressed by the display of emotion taking over.

"You should go lie down," Ramsey said, marking the visual down as something to make note of in his journal. "Some rest will help. I'll make us something to eat."

Adam opened its mouth as if it was going to say something, and then it must have changed its mind. The creature turned towards the bedroom but only made it halfway down the hall before it collapsed. As large as it was, the emotion's wracking its body must have been too big for it to handle. The creature's tears splattered against the wooden floor, and it was only able to crawl forward a few more steps, barely making it to the door, before it gave up and curled into a ball. Its horrendous, hoarse sobs resonated off the walls worse than Wisp's howling ever did. Ramsey ground his teeth in irritation, but he left the creature alone and went into the kitchen to work.

# CHAPTER FIFTEEN

There was not much food left in the cabinets. Ramsey dreaded the idea of venturing to the store under the present circumstances, so he forced himself to get creative. He threw canned spinach, brown rice, and mushrooms together and called it dinner. He set it out in plastic bowls and called Adam to the table, but the damn creature did not move.

Ramsey waited for a full fifteen minutes before leaving the kitchen to look for Adam. He found it curled up in Mildred Abernathy's bed, buried under a pile of blankets that had been pulled up from their neat, tucked-in corners and now barely covered its feet.

Ramsey walked over to the bed and put his hand on the creature's shoulder.

"Adam," he said. "It is time for dinner."

"I don't want to eat." The creature's muttering was barely audible.

"You have to." Ramsey wasn't above grabbing the side of the mattress and tipping the creature out onto the floor. "You're no good to anyone at all if you are weak."

Adam growled and smashed the covers further up against its face. "If I'm no good, you can un-make me, then," it said.

Ramsey rolled his eyes and pinched the bridge of his nose. "I am not doing this with you," he said. "You came from the grave; you were born from it. For all that I am amazed by your weak stomach for a little gore. You will have to steel yourself to death, because it is everywhere."

"I'm not eating." Adam's only response was more defiant than before.

"Fine." Ramsey pulled away. "Your dinner is on the table. It's up to you when you decide that your hunger strike is over. If it collects maggots in the meantime, you still won't have anything else until it is eaten."

Adam made a short, noncommittal sound. Ramsey left the bedroom and shut the door behind him, thoroughly fed-up.

'*R*amsey.' Wisp's voice was the sound of long strips of wallpaper being peeled up. Hearing the ghost, as he was used to hearing it, was strangely comforting. Ramsey was already only half-asleep, and the ghost pulled him back into full consciousness.

"Mm?" Ramsey rubbed the back of his neck and shifted his hips.

'*Your creature is not resting,*' the ghost sighed. '*It is not sleeping. Wretched thing.*'

"It seems that no one under this roof is going to be permitted any sleep," Ramsey said. He slipped out from under his covers and made his way through the darkness towards the line of yellow light that seeped underneath his bedroom door. When he opened the door, the light hit his eyes and made him wince. The hall and the kitchen lights were on, as well as the light in his mother's bedroom. Ramsey sucked on his teeth in frustration and stepped into the hall.

"Adam!" He set his hand against the wall and peered around, into the kitchen. "Adam, what are you doing with all these lights on? You can't be afraid of the dark." How ironic that would be. The creature was nowhere to be seen when Ramsey walked in, but the bowl on the dining table was empty. For half a second, before he moved into the bedroom, he was struck with paranoia. Ramsey took a detour and went to check the front door, grabbing the handle and jerking it to make sure that it was still locked. It stuck fast, reassuring him that its bolt was still in place. Even with that, he still had visions of Adam making its way through the front yard and across the wooden walkways that led to the main street. There was no telling, then, who would run into it first. And if the wildlife did not find a way to claim it, then the God-fearing, superstitious swamp-dwellers would set it on fire within minutes. Not one of them would know a scientific marvel if it bit them in the ass.

Ramsey put himself back on course towards his mother's bedroom. The light was on in the bathroom, too, and he caught a glimpse of the creature's face in the mirror above her broken sink. Ramsey let out a breath that he could only identify as relief and then stood in the bathroom door, spreading his arms to block the entire entryway.

"What are you doing?" Ramsey demanded. The creature looked at him. It was not wearing any clothes, and its hair was completely undone, tumbling past its shoulders. From where he was standing, the only eye that Ramsey could see was the milk-white one.

"I ate," the creature said. Ramsey waited for more, and when nothing else was said, he urged for more details.

"It is late at night, and you are walking around leaving every light on in this house." He raised his chin. "Are you scared of the dark?"

"Yes," Adam said, without a single lick of shame. It turned its face back towards the mirror, a frown pulling down the corners of its mouth. "I am...all wrong."

"What do you mean?" It was too late at night and Ramsey was too tired to rehash any part of this discussion intelligently.

"Did you know that I was going to be like this?" The creature kept going. "Or...is it my fault? It has to be. You don't make mistakes."

Ramsey slid his arm down the door frame and stood a little taller. "You are just as you are meant to be," he said. "And you need to go to sleep. That is something you must get used to again, just like everything else. Falling asleep at night and waking back up in the morning."

Adam heaved a deep sigh and then nodded. "Can I leave a light on?" it asked.

"One light," Ramsey said. "The bathroom light. I am turning off the rest." Since dressing the creature in his own clothes, he had not taken a good look at its form. Now, he had to admit to himself that he was impressed by his own work. Everything looked like it belonged together, every piece in such beautiful symmetry as if he had crafted the flesh out of clay. Maybe there was more to be salvaged than he initially thought—which was a boon, considering Abel's body was no longer within reach.

When his gaze returned to Adam's face, the creature was looking up at him with such deep sorrow in that singular green eye that Ramsey was taken aback.

"Could you stay with me?" the creature asked. Ramsey shook his head.

"No," he said. "I am going back to my own bed." He could only imagine what it would be like, trying to cozy up to something large and ungainly in such a narrow bed. Besides that, Adam's smell had only *slightly* dissipated, and the room still reeked. He would have to come up with a fix for that, but not tonight.

"All right." Adam turned its head. "I am sorry that I woke you."

"Just go to sleep," Ramsey said. "That is all I want."

158

# CHAPTER SIXTEEN

R amsey did not return to bed. When he left his mother's bedroom, he pulled the door shut behind him again and turned off the hall and the kitchen lights on his way through. He paused at his brother's door, and everything in him screamed that he should move on. Yet, he couldn't shake the feeling that his dream from a few days ago had left him with, and he wondered if the room was in really such bad shape.

He waited to see if Wisp's voice would intervene, or if something else would happen by way of divine intervention to change his course. All he was met with was a quiet house.

Ramsey pulled the key down from its resting place on top of the door frame and unlocked the door. Immediately, he was hit the smell of old laundry and rotten food that had been baking together in Louisiana heat. He flicked the light on and a roach ran by his foot before vanishing underneath the bed.

His brother's room was worse than what had been shown to him in his dream. The bedcovers had been stripped off, at some point, and all the old papers and photos were on the floor, tangled up in a burgundy comforter. The stained white sheets were covered in old food and debris, and there was only one pillow still on the bed with the center sunken in, as if someone had been napping on it up until recently. The mirror was still mounted on the wall, however. Ramsey thought that was an interesting detail. He saw his own gaunt face, and then his gaze drifted towards the reflected headboard, where something else was hovering.

At first, it just looked like his shadow; but the longer that Ramsey looked, the more definite a shape it took. One moment it was an ominous and vague black shape, and then it was fully Abel, standing with their cigarette holder and wearing a broad-brimmed sunhat that scooped down towards their nose.

Ramsey jumped and turned around, but when he looked at the bed, there was nothing. He turned, slowly, to face the mirror again—and Abel was still there.

"Hello, doctor," they said. Their voice brushed across his ear as if they were standing right by his shoulder. "Is your busy mind still going?"

Ramsey watched his own larynx bob as he swallowed. "I knew that you are not what you seem," he said. "Are you even really dead?"

"Are you even still alive?" Abel's reflection moved a little closer to his. "That's a better question. I am surprised you haven't started questioning your own sanity with all this, Doctor Abernathy. Of course, if I was you, I would have started questioning myself a lot sooner." Their reflection placed out the cigarette on Ramsey's neck, and he jumped at the sting. He swatted at his neck like he was killing a fly, but the only thing his fingers smacked was a raw burn.

"I am sane," Ramsey hissed, glaring daggers at their reflection.

"Sane men don't speak to ghosts." Abel clucked their tongue. "Sane men don't move dead bodies around the house and pretend that they're alive." They slid their hands over his shoulders, and Ramsey jerked again.

"Oh," Abel cooed. "I know that isn't what you want. My apologies." They moved to his other side, their reflection disappearing behind his own for only half a second. They reappeared over his other shoulder with a new face, one that was all too familiar.

It was Victor, or what *looked* like Victor, but the smile was all Abel. They tilted their head and rested it against Ramsey's shoulder, trailing their hand down the front of his chest.

"That's better," Abel said. "That's what you like to see, isn't it? That's the face you have been working for this whole time." Their other hand snaked around Ramsey's hip and plunged down the front of his pants. When he looked down, the fabric wasn't even moving, but he still felt their fingers stroking his cock to life.

Ramsey made a wordless sound and put his hand down to cover his crotch. "You..." He ground his teeth. "Fuck you."

"I don't think that's what you want. I'm still trying to figure out your tastes." Abel's voice with Victor's face taunted him through the mirror. "Oh, but I think I know, now." They kept their hand on his cock, still moving their fingers up and down and stroking the sensitive shaft. They moved again, temporarily vanishing behind him before reappearing over the shoulder where they had started, and this time they were wearing Adam's face.

Ramsey wanted to bolt, but he was frozen in place. His cock was alive and throbbing, and he could not tear his eyes away from Adam's reflection in the mirror. Their expression shifted until it was no longer a self-satisfied grin, and became instead the creature's permanently mournful expression.

Ramsey's knees trembled, but Abel held him close against their chest to keep him upright. Sweat raced down the sides of his face and dripped off the tip of his nose. Ramsey reached down and grabbed himself. In the mirror, their fingers overlapped, but no one else was touching him outside of the reflection. He pumped his shaft, and the pressure around his shoulders released, allowing him to drop to his knees. Ramsey leaned over, stroking himself, thrusting into his own hand to try and bring himself relief—*any* relief, because now everything was pounding, including his head.

He thought of Adam—specifically Adam's expression paired with the exhilaration of the moment Ramsey brought the shovel down on Abel's neck. Never had he felt so powerful before, so entirely in control. Ramsey bit his bottom lip and exhaled so hard through his nose that it dripped. He came onto the comforter that was bunched-up on the floor, so hard and so much that it was almost concerning.

Ramsey set both hands against the floor and sat there for a minute, catching his breath. His semen had landed right onto a wrinkled photo of Victor and his mother, splattered right between them.

Ramsey made a face and picked up the photo, wiping it off on his pant leg.

"Are you all right?" Adam's voice came from the doorway. Ramsey whipped his head around to see the creature standing there, still not dressed, and swaying on its feet as if it had been pulled out of a deep sleep.

"Fucking...Christ on a cross!" Ramsey pinched the bridge of his nose. "You do not listen, do you?"

"I'm sorry," Adam said quietly. "I heard a strange noise and I thought...you were crying."

"No." Ramsey still did not move to stand up, not with his dick hanging out from his pants. "I am not crying. I *should* be crying, because God knows that I can't get you to listen to me worth a damn."

"I'm sorry," Adam said again. "I'll go to bed."

"Come here." Ramsey heard his own voice, but it wasn't coming from his mouth. He grabbed the end of the bed to pull himself up, twisting around and trying to put himself back to decency at the same time.

Adam stepped further into the room, a cautious expression on its face. Ramsey caught a glimpse of a second body, one that looked like a hazy mirror version of his own, and he heard his own voice again.

"I'm sorry, Adam," the voice said. "Come here. I want to show you something."

"No, goddammit! I am right here!" Ramsey stood and lunged, intending to block Adam from reaching this thing that was impersonating him. He reached out to grab a fistful of chestnut hair that was too much like his own and yanked. The entity twisted and snarled, but when it turned around, he found himself staring into Adam's face, and not his own. There was no one else in the room. The Adam standing by the door smiled at him, waved, and vanished within the blink of an eye.

Adam fell, and Ramsey landed on top of it. The creature thrashed and tried to buck him off, but Ramsey brought his open hand down across its face before grabbing it by the throat. The blow stunned Adam into silence, and for a moment, Ramsey just lay there on top of the creature. He squeezed its throat until he felt its pulse hammering against his fingers. Strong, for something that had only been alive for a few days.

He stared into Adam's face while he squeezed, waiting to see if it would turn colors, or if the creature would even be aware enough of what was coming to try and fight him off again. He wondered if Adam would just lay there and accept its fate, let Ramsey kill it—and the thought made him hard. He was so stiff, actually, that he suddenly couldn't focus on anything else.

Adam choked, and that brought Ramsey back to the moment—to the creature's throat in his hands, its *life* in his hands. The life he gave it, to begin with. And if anyone should have the right to take it back, it should be him.

Adam's fist collided with Ramsey's throat, and he heard his own windpipe crinkle. Ramsey gagged and let go, crawling backward off the monster until he was on the floor.

Ramsey fought for his own breath. He looked up at the creature from his position on all fours, while Adam towered over him with its fists balled up at its side.

"You wish I was dead!" Adam's words were saturated with hurt and betrayal that Ramsey did not even realize it was capable of expressing. "You tried to kill me!"

"No," Ramsey corrected, still gasping while sitting up more on his knees. "I...was not...trying to kill you!" He touched his own throat, and it felt like it was on fire.

In the background, he heard clanging and clattering that sounded like it was coming from the kitchen. Wisp throwing a tantrum, but for what reason, now? Ramsey's headache grew, wrapping around the entire back of his skull like a metal band.

*'Ruined!'* Wisp's screams were like a distant whistling kettle. *'Ruined! Ruined!'*

"Why?" Tears rolled down Adam's cheeks, springing off its chin like raindrops sliding down a gutter. "Why do you hate me so much? I am what you *created!*" More tears. "Even if I'm not what you *wanted!*"

Ramsey tried, again, to stand, but he did not get very far before Adam grabbed him by the hair and started dragging him across the floor. He had not realized, until that moment, just how strong his creature was.

Under any other circumstances, he might have been thrilled.

"Adam!" Ramsey caught his breath enough to snap. "Let me go!" He tried to roll back onto all fours and regain control, to wrench himself away, but Adam was hauling him too quickly. Ramsey's scalp and his neck both burned.

"I wanted you to love me." Adam's tears made its anger sound that much sharper. "But you were so, so quick to *hate* me, and to *kill*—I think that's all you know how to do!" Adam made it all the way to the hallway before it dropped Ramsey to the floor. Ramsey watched its feet disappear into the kitchen and he started crawling towards the front door, fighting the searing pain in his legs and his back.

"Christ on a cross," Adam said, a perfect imitation of Ramsey's own intonation. Something heavy and metal slammed into the back of Ramsey's head, and he tasted blood.

"What the fuck are you doing?" Ramsey spat onto the floor. The metal collided with his head again, and his vision started swimming.

"It doesn't feel good!" Adam shouted, although it sounded more like the creature intended it as a question. "It doesn't! Feel! Good!" With every new word, it slammed the metal into Ramsey's head. With each blow, Ramsey tasted more blood and darkness crept across his vision.

"Adam!" He tried one more time to talk the creature down from its frenzy. "Adam, please!"

A merciful pause. Ramsey lie prostrate on the floor with his hands pressed against the wood, blood and saliva leaking out of his mouth, unable to see anything other than the faintest pinprick of light.

Over the ringing in his ears, Adam was bawling.

"I can't," the creature sobbed. "I don't want to."

"You really are too good for him," Abel's voice joined the chaos, and Ramsey's stomach twisted so hard it audibly gargled.

———————

"I don't know what to do," Adam said, pitifully. "I don't know what to do, I don't want to hurt him anymore. I didn't want to hurt him at all."

"I know," Abel said, gentle and humoring. Metal came to rest against the back of Ramsey's neck. "But when you live in the bayou, there are some things you just can't take a chance with. Like when you don't know whether a snake is going to bite you, it's best not to take the chance."

The creature paused. "What about his brother?"

Ramsey could barely hear the response. "We can sew the head back on," Abel said.

And that was the last Ramsey heard before his vision tunneled completely.

# CHAPTER SEVENTEEN

When Ramsey's vision returned, the world had been painted over in black and white. He only knew this because he was staring at his roof, at his ceiling fan, and everything was in shades of grey. Possible, he supposed, because of how hard he'd been hit over the head. Ramsey expected himself to be in too much pain to move, but when he went to turn onto his side, it was the exact opposite. If anything, he moved now like all his joints had been greased.

'*We can sew the head back on,*' Ramsey remembered the words and touched his throat. There were no stitches, and no gash. He was right as rain, aside from his vision.

Ramsey sat up in bed and looked around. Everything was untouched, as far as he could tell. The door was open, and the hallway light was on. Ramsey pushed out an exasperated exhale and stood up.

He started to call for Adam, but the words would not form. They got stuck in his throat like a stone and the only sound that came out of his mouth was a raspy hiss. Ramsey paused, mortified, and tried again. He set his hand against the base of his throat, as if somehow that would help, but the same sound was all that came out again.

Ramsey tried to make any noise at all, but he couldn't so much as click his tongue off his teeth. Panic ignited in his chest and Ramsey began staggering towards the hall, still trying to talk, to scream—*anything.*

"That is pretty good," Adam's voice came from the kitchen. "It looks better than it did yesterday. You should have seen my handwriting, when Abel first started teaching me."

"My hands feel useless," Ramsey's voice answered, but it didn't sound *quite* like him. There was something wrong about it—other than the fact that it wasn't coming *from him.*

Ramsey came to a stop in the kitchen entrance and stood there, staring, unable to believe what he was seeing. Adam hovered near the table, wearing Ramsey's old clothes, a plain dark t-shirt that came up a little too high over their long torso and a pair of dark jeans. Ramsey's body sat in one of the wooden chairs, with the back of his head facing the entrance and his brown curly hair matted with blood. Adam looked up, and Ramsey's body twisted in the chair, glancing over his shoulder.

His face was bruised all to hell. It looked like he had been hit head-on with a car. But the bruises were healing, and there was an ugly scar across his throat. The stitches were done in black thread, and the edges of the gash were stapled where the thread had not been sufficient.

Suddenly, Ramsey was cold, and his face tingled like he was about to pass out—but somehow knew that he wouldn't.

"What is it?" Ramsey's head was turned at such an unnatural angle that it looked like it was about to fall off.

"I think we have a visitor." Adam let out a breath and added with a whisper, "finally."

"Oh." Ramsey's brow crinkled. "Is he going to throw a fit?"

"Probably." Adam shrugged. It turned back to what looked like a homemade worksheet with some letters scribbled onto drawn lines. "I will tell Abel when they come back."

"Well," Ramsey's body said, with no small amount of vicious glee, "if he starts throwing things, all the dishes are plastic."

Adam smiled but didn't respond. Ramsey stumbled back a step and put his hand to his head, trying to understand what was happening, what this *meant*.

Ramsey turned away from the scene and started running towards the front door. It was open, too. He didn't know *why*. What was Adam doing, leaving all the doors open, and the lights on everywhere? Ramsey ran out onto the porch, heading for the stairs, but then was stopped in his tracks by a full-body blow like he had run into a wall.

Ramsey fell to his knees at the top of the stairs and looked out across the front yard. Branches swaying in the light afternoon breeze cast dappled patterns onto the ground, and over the water, a heron caught a fish in its bill.

Still, none of it was in color.

Close to the bank, the water rippled. Ramsey watched as the water parted and rolled across the back of an enormous dark alligator. The alligator waddled onto the dirt and opened its monstrous jaws, displaying ragged teeth. Something came rolling out from the depths of its throat, something white and spongy and covered in grime. It landed on the ground and Ramsey recognized it as a head; the same head that he had left in its coffin, the one that had followed him after the storm.

Ramsey set his hands on his knees and heaved. He wished he could throw up. He wished he could cry. Nothing came when he tried. All he could do was make those ugly, wretched hissing sounds.

Behind him, from within the house, Adam spoke again.

"I'm going to close this door, Victor, there's a gator in the yard."

WHAT
CREATES
MONSTE

# Adam

SIRIUS

*'Every day, he gets farther away.'*

Adam paused, staring at the notepad in front of him. His large, unwieldy handwriting staggered over the topmost line, clumsy and unrefined. He wished that he could learn better from Abel, whose handwriting was flawless—loops and curls and elegant lines that flowed together to create seamless, straight rows. Centuries of practice, Abel reassured him with a kiss on the temple. Yet, the concept of *centuries* was still beyond Adam's comprehension.

It had appeared in one of their romance novels. The hero pulled his heroine close and whispered, "I will love you for centuries". Adam understood that it meant a very, very long time. But to him, 'a long time' was still waiting in the long shadows of the afternoon for night to finally settle in. 'A long time' was waiting for the sun to rise on the nights he couldn't sleep, since he was still not brave enough to explore the swamp and everything it had to offer.

Abel reassured him that there was so much to see, that the night was far from boring as it seemed just sitting in the house. They told Adam that when he was ready, they would take him to see the streets of New Orleans, where there would be music and delicious food and many, many bright and sparkling lights.

Adam wasn't so sure about all that. But if Abel wanted him to go, he would go.

*'I want to be him.'*

His words continued down to the next line, bigger than before, although a little bit neater. He wished, more than anything, that he could keep his hand from shaking when he wrote. However, there was no telling if that particular problem would ever heal, the more his brain caught up to his body.

*'I know that is terrible.'*

Even now, it was difficult to encapsulate exactly *how* he knew his father was bad. Rage and violence were what Dr. Abernathy carried, it was all he had balled up in his chest and the only way he could express his feelings. Adam had been able to sense that from the beginning, and yet hoped he could untangle it, somehow. Maybe that was selfishness on his part from wanting to fill the hole in his own chest. The hole that he wanted fatherly affection to fill, but he did not deserve it, so of course he had not received it—it was all pure greed. After all, was the act of creation not the ultimate expression of love? Was the fact that Adam even existed not enough? He should have been grateful and left it all at that. The expectation to look into the face of his creator and see anything other than indifference was putting too much onto a man who was already overburdened, who had already pushed himself to the brink of his own sanity to give Adam the greatest gift of life.

Adam wanted to *be* him, to emulate his creator because then, if he could harness that greatness for himself, he could fill the void on his own and not have to reach for another to do so.

And then maybe, just maybe, he would understand why Dr. Abernathy hated him so much. Why there was bitterness in his eyes and the thin line of his mouth when he looked Adam up and down. These were all things that Adam had resigned himself to never understanding, because Dr. Abernathy was dead, and Adam did not have the tools to create a new life.

The body that *was* the doctor's now belonged to his brother, Victor—whom Adam had only known as the ghost Wisp for quite some time. Victor was newer to life than Adam, but older in consciousness. His mind adapted faster, or maybe it was that his body was better connected, on account that it was mostly in one piece. His handwriting was certainly better, even though it was boxy and crooked. Abel praised his progress just as much as they praised Adam's, and for some reason, that nettled.

A yellow-gloved hand descended over Adam's shoulder and picked up the notepad before he was finished. Adam made a face, but he didn't protest.

"Look at how nicely you're doing," Abel said from behind him. Adam shifted in his seat and slumped over the table, putting his head onto his arms. Abel rubbed his back.

"'I know that is terrible.' Why do you say that?" Abel asked.

Adam shrugged. "He hurt you," he said. His own voice echoed around his ears, bouncing off the table's surface. "He hurt me, he...was not a nice man."

"No," Abel agreed. "But you have to bear this in mind, my darling. There is no such thing as a 'nice man.'" They set the paper pad back down. "There are only men who act selfishly, and selfless men who act against their own interests, most often to a fault."

"Which one am I?" Adam asked.

"You are too new to worry about labels, dear." Adam tapped the paper pad. "Keep going."

Adam straightened in his chair and Abel's fingertips raked gently over his temples, dragging his wild hair back and away from his face. "Maybe I can be one," he said. "The first one."

"The first what?" Abel mused.

"The first good man," Adam stared at his paper. "It isn't impossible, is it?"

"You are impossible, by your very existence, and yet here you are," Abel said. "I see no reason why you can't be the first genuinely good person in the world. Although even the saints hit their stumbling blocks, so I would say you are in for a long road."

"I still want to try," Adam said. At this point, he was also stalling, because his hand was shaking so badly that it was difficult to hold his pen.

"We will work on your letters, first," Abel said. "Then you can worry about being good, or nice, or whatever it is your heart desires."

"Are they different?" Adam asked.

"Very," Abel told him. "Nice and good are nowhere near the same. Nice is subjective, goodness is inherent." Abel tapped Adam's shoulder. "Three more sentences, please. And then you can help me make dinner."

Adam swallowed. "Yes, mama," he said quietly.

# ABOUT THE AUTHOR

SIRIUS (they/them) is the author of The Dread South Series, the Gentleman Demon series, the Wirekillers series, the Draonir Saga, and multiple short stories included in various anthologies and literary magazines. When not writing, they are spreading blasphemy as a drag king or doting on their beloved dogs.